THE TEXAS TATTLER

All The News You Need To Know...And More!

We all heard rumors that Wyatt Brody had been plotting to help his brother marry the Texas senior senator's daughter. He'd even gone so far as to "visit" Alexis Cavanaugh multiple times—wining and dining her in elaborate establishments. But when Lance Brody up and married his mousy secretary, it *seemed* that the Brody/Cavanaugh merger was off.

Now, rumors abound that the still-eligible Brody brother is back romancing Miss Cavanaugh. Could there have been more to their meetings than one might have imagined? Perhaps the Cavanaughs are so desperate to marry into the Brody family it doesn't matter which brother the groom is! Though we can certainly attest to Wyatt Brody's appeal—the man is quite the charmer. Or...could there be something to that noticeable "bump" beginning to appear at Alexis's middle? Perhaps a Brody heir is on the way?

Dear Reader,

Welcome to book four of the TEXAS CATTLEMAN'S CLUB: MAVERICK COUNTY MILLIONAIRES series—the story of oilman Wyatt Brody and Alexis Cavanaugh!

As far as I'm concerned, the only thing sexier than a man who knows exactly what he wants is a man who thinks he does, then realizes he's wrong. That sums up Wyatt. He has it all figured out. At least he thinks he does, then Alexis comes along and turns all of his perfectly engineered plans upside down.

Alexis is a woman on a mission. She knows what she wants, and she's willing to go to any lengths to get it. Until she realizes that what she wants may not be worth the price she has to pay.

These two put me through so many emotional twists and turns I nearly wound up with whiplash! But in the end it was more than worth it.

I hope you enjoy their story as much as I did!

Michelle Celmer

MICHELLE CELMER

THE OILMAN'S BABY BARGAIN

Published by Silhouette Books
America's Publisher of Contemporary Romance

Special thanks and acknowledgment to Michelle Celmer
for her contribution to the Texas Cattleman's Club:
Maverick County Millionaires miniseries.

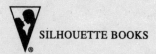 SILHOUETTE BOOKS

ISBN-13: 978-0-373-76970-4

Recycling programs
for this product may
not exist in your area.

THE OILMAN'S BABY BARGAIN

Visit Silhouette Books at www.eHarlequin.com

Printed in U.S.A.

MICHELLE CELMER

Bestselling author Michelle Celmer lives in southeastern Michigan with her husband, their three children, two dogs and two cats. When she's not writing or busy being a mom, you can find her in the garden or curled up with a romance novel. And if you twist her arm real hard you can usually persuade her into a day of power shopping.

Michelle loves to hear from readers. Visit her Web site at www.michellecelmer.com, or write her at P.O. Box 300, Clawson, MI 48017.

Texas Cattleman's Club: Maverick County Millionaires

One

Alexis Cavanaugh was in love with the wrong brother.

She gazed across the candlelit table at the man she had spent the better part of the past week in D.C. with, only half listening as he spoke fervently about Brody Oil and Gas, the company he co-owned with his brother Lance. The brother she was *supposed* to be marrying.

Not that she had expected to fall in love with Lance. The marriage was little more than a business deal cooked up by the Brody brothers and her father, Bruce Cavanaugh, senior senator from her home state of Texas. But hadn't she always done what her father asked of her? Didn't he, as he'd always claimed, know what was best? A marriage to Lance would provide her the financial security and station in society that she'd earned—although other than possess the Cavanaugh name, she wasn't sure what she'd ever done to deserve it.

Not that she didn't find Lance appealing. He was tall and dark and devastatingly attractive—not to mention built like a tank—with a charm that drew people to him. A gentle giant. But he wasn't as refined a man as she was accustomed to. He seemed more comfortable among the roughnecks at the refinery than the shareholders. Mitch, on the other hand, had seemed perfectly at ease with the elite of D.C. They had attended half a dozen parties and fundraisers together—Mitch on his brother's behalf, of course—and he could schmooze with the best of them. He was clearly the brains behind Brody Oil and Gas.

And the brother she clearly was falling for.

So many men treated her like a brainless, witless showpiece. Better seen and not heard. But Mitch listened to her. He *heard* her, and seemed genuinely interested in what she had to say.

She realized suddenly that he was meeting her gaze across the table, a grin on his ridiculously handsome face. A face that had become quite familiar over the past few days. She had memorized every line and curve, the slope of his nose, the sensual shape of his chocolate-brown eyes, the fullness of his lips and sharp set of his jaw. She knew every expression and nuance. And the smile he wore now was an amused one.

"What?" she asked.

"You haven't heard a word I've said, have you?"

He was right. He'd been talking about his business, which obviously meant more to him than anything else, and she had completely zoned out. In her own defense, it was tough to watch those full lips move and not become entranced, not be lulled by the deep tenor of his voice. But that was no excuse to be rude. She was usually an exceptional listener.

"I'm sorry," she apologized.

"I'm the one who should be apologizing. I'm obviously boring you to death. I forget that not everyone is as passionate as I am about the oil business."

"I enjoy hearing you talk about it. I guess I'm just a little tired. It's been a very busy week."

"It has," Mitch agreed, with a smile that was just this side of seductive. "My brother has no idea what he's missing."

Did he feel the same connection, the same longing for her that she had for him? Or was he simply being polite? Was he just naturally flirtatious, like his brother?

"It's late. I should get you back to the hotel."

Just for a moment, she let herself believe that he

couldn't wait to get her back to her room so he could make passionate love to her. The idea both thrilled and terrified her. She had always hoped her first time would be special, and she knew without a doubt that with Mitch, it would be.

But that wasn't going to happen because she was marrying his brother. And shouldn't she save something as precious as her virginity for her spouse? Even if it wasn't a real marriage?

He summoned the waiter and paid the exorbitantly high bill without batting an eyelash. What did she expect when he took her to the most exclusive restaurant in D.C.? Money was obviously of no concern.

He helped her up from her seat and walked her to the door. She took pleasure in the way every head in the room swiveled in his direction. Men watched with envy as their female companions swooned, eyes filled with silent longing.

Sorry, girls, he's all mine. At least until she became officially engaged to Lance. If only she could capture this time and make it last forever. Make a life with Mitch instead of Lance.

The limo was already waiting for them as they stepped out into the hot and muggy evening air, but the soft leather felt cool as she slipped inside. "The Watergate Hotel," Mitch told the driver.

She hoped they would talk more on the way there, but his cell phone rang. He checked the display and told her, "Sorry, but I have to take this."

Though he said nothing specific, it was clear by his tone that the conversation had something to do with the fire at the refinery. She'd heard from her father that the investigation pointed to arson, and though there were no solid suspects, rumors were spreading that Lance's rival, Alejandro Montoya, might be responsible. She couldn't understand why anyone would put so many lives in danger, but having grown up around politics, she'd learned that some people were capable of terrible things.

Mitch disconnected just as the limo pulled up to the hotel. Usually they parted ways in the lobby, as their rooms were in different wings, but tonight Mitch offered to accompany her to her door.

He was just being polite, she told herself. But why now? Why was tonight any different than the last?

The air seemed to sizzle with electricity as they rode the elevator up to the penthouse. More than usual she felt acutely aware of his presence beside her. Or maybe it was just her imagination.

When the doors slid open, he touched her waist to lead her out. His hand felt huge, and warmth seeped through the silk of her sundress, making the skin beneath tingle. She couldn't recall him touching her this way before, and she was sure she would have noticed. When they reached her door, he took the key from her and opened it. She stepped inside and he leaned against the jamb.

"I had a nice time tonight, Lexi," he said. There was heat in his eyes as they searched her face, then drifted lower, to the front of her dress, where, thanks to her very expensive and uncomfortable push-up bra, her breasts swelled over and begged to be noticed. He did notice, and he obviously liked what he saw.

She had never been one to play the seductress, but tonight she was feeling the part. Would it hurt her, for the first time in her boring and proper life, to do something scandalous and wicked? Something just for herself? Who, besides the two of them, would ever know? After years of chastity, hadn't she earned one night of unbridled passion and ecstasy?

She knew without a doubt he would give her exactly that.

"I had a nice time, too," she said, gazing up at him through the fringe of her lashes, wearing what she hoped was a seductive smile. Maybe it was the wine, or the candlelit dinner, but she could feel her inhibitions melting away. "Would you like to come inside for a nightcap?"

Without hesitation he stepped into the room, closing the door behind him. She opened her mouth to ask him what he wanted to drink, but before she could make a sound his arms were around her, drawing her against him. Her nipples tingled almost painfully as they pressed against the wall of his chest and her knees went weak with excitement. Then he lowered his head and kissed her. Her lips parted with a surprised gasp, and he dipped in for a taste.

She expected him to plunder and dominate the way the men did in her favorite romance novels. Instead, his lips were soft and gentle, his touch tender. In spite of having wanted this with all of her heart, she was so stunned she was actually kissing her future brother-in-law that she stood stiff in his arms.

He must have interpreted her reaction as a rejection, because he released her and pulled away. "I'm sorry," he said. "But I've been fantasizing about doing that all night. All *week*."

So had she, and she wasn't going to blow it. She wasn't going to let her fear of the unknown ruin this chance for a night with the man of her dreams.

She grinned her most wicked smile and slid her hands up his chest, wrapping them around his neck. "Then why did you stop?"

This time when he kissed her, he didn't stop. And when he took her to bed, he proved to be everything she had imagined.

And more.

Last night had been the most amazing, terrifying and wonderful night of Lexi's life. She'd had no idea two people could connect—could be in perfect sync—the way she and Mitch had been. She had tried to hide the fact that she was a virgin, but of course he'd figured it out. She'd worried that he might be angry or put off, but the opposite had been true. He'd been so sweet and gentle with her. What could have been a painful, awkward experience had been more beautiful than she had ever imagined possible.

The instant she woke the next morning, cradled in a cocoon of warm silk sheets that still held the scent of Mitch's aftershave, she knew without a doubt that she wouldn't be marrying Lance. She wanted Mitch. And she was sure that if she pleaded her case to her father, he would see that the other Brody brother would be a much better match. As far as he was concerned, it was only the Brody name that was important.

Before she even opened her eyes she smiled to herself and began to imagine what life would be like married to Mitch. How happy she would be because they would love each other. She imagined what their children would look like. They would have a son who would be tall and fit with Mitch's dark hair, olive tones and striking features, and a girl, pretty and graceful with Lexi's creamy complexion and blond hair.

They would have a ceremony in the garden at her father's Houston estate, then honeymoon somewhere warm and exotic. Maybe Cabo San Lucas, or the Bahamas. And if Mitch was agreeable, they could try to conceive while they were there. What better time to get pregnant than on her honeymoon? She had always wanted to be a mother, to have at least three or four children.

Lexi heard movement in the room and realized Mitch was already up. She peered at the clock on the bedside table, surprised to find that it was barely 7:00 a.m.

"Are you awake?" Mitch asked.

She rolled to face him, ready to smile and say, *why don't you climb back in bed and find out,* but he was already showered and dressed, and when she saw the look on his face, her heart sank. Then she realized, of course he would look distressed. He was about to steal his brother's fiancée. Maybe he thought she loved Lance.

She sat up, holding the sheet against her bare breasts. "Good morning."

"We need to talk," he said.

She nodded, barely able to contain her excitement. Here it comes. He was going to tell her he loved her, and beg her to marry him instead of Lance. Of course she would say yes. Then he would undress, and climb back into bed, and she would spend the rest of the morning showing him just how much she loved him. Then everything would be perfect, just like the happily-ever-afters in the romance novels.

His expression somber, he said, "I don't suppose I have to tell you that we've made a drastic mistake."

Wait, what?

A *mistake?*

She had to replay the words several times in her mind, convinced she must have misunderstood.

"No one can ever know that this happened," he continued, his tone grim. "Especially my brother."

He might as well have reached into her chest and ripped out her heart, because that was the way it felt. The fierce, hollow ache was nearly unbearable.

For years she had endured her father's criticism and indifference. No matter what she did to please him, however closely she played by his rules, it was never enough to win his love. Now, once again, she had been rejected by a man whose affection she desperately craved.

Maybe there was something wrong with her, something that made her unlovable.

"Lance is flying in this afternoon to officially propose," Mitch told her. "You have to pretend that everything is fine, and nothing has changed."

How could she act as though everything was fine when she was falling apart? And how could she have been so stupid? Why didn't she see that it was just sex to him? Maybe it was some sort of warped sibling rivalry. Maybe Mitch seduced all of his brother's girlfriends.

Humiliation burned her from the inside out, but she would die before she let Mitch know.

She lifted her nose at him and pasted on a look of boredom. "I don't have to pretend everything is fine,

Mitch. As far as I'm concerned, things are great. You definitely served your purpose."

He frowned. "What purpose was that?"

She racked her brain, grasping for the worst, most awful thing she could possibly say to hurt him as much as he'd hurt her. "A cheap thrill, to cheat my arranged husband out of my virginity. And who better to do it with than his brother. Although I'm sorry to say, I expected better. Your performance wasn't exactly earth-shattering."

Mitch's expression went from one of confusion to ice-cold hatred. She waited for him to shout and berate her, the way her father often did when he was displeased with her. But all he said was, "I should have expected as much from a spoiled and pampered heiress."

No words could have stung more or cut deeper.

He grabbed his wallet from the bedside table. "Meet me downstairs in the lounge at noon," he said, then turned and left without another word.

She sat there for several minutes, feeling sick with grief, but then she began to feel something else. She began to feel angry. How dare he play with her emotions that way. How dare he make love to her and take from her the most precious gift she had to offer—her innocence—then ruthlessly reject her.

Well, she would show him. She would marry his brother and she would make Lance love her. She would be the best wife, the best mother—everything Lance could ever want in a mate.

Mitch would see how happy they were, see how perfect she could be, and he would regret letting her go for the rest of his life.

Two

Mitchell Brody had never been one to compromise, but when it came to Brody Oil and Gas, he would do just about anything to ensure its continued growth and success. Even if that meant marrying a spoiled, heartless, manipulative heiress who had a block of ice where her heart belonged.

Bruce Cavanaugh glared at Mitch from behind his massive desk—the desk he boasted once belonged to JFK—in his Houston office, where he sat like a king addressing a lowly peasant. Everything in the room, from the rich furnishings to his many accolades framed and hung on the walls, was designed to intimidate. Mitch would happily tell the overbearing son of a bitch to go to hell, but unfortunately, he and Lance needed his senatorial support. Even more so since the fire at the refinery. If they planned to keep profits up, they needed to expand.

"Your brother has humiliated my family," he told Mitch.

"I know he has, sir. Once more, I would like to express our deepest apologies."

"Rejecting my Lexi for a lowly secretary," he scoffed, as if Kate's profession somehow made her unworthy. Mitch wondered how the senator would feel if he knew that while she was supposed to be planning a wedding with Lance, his precious daughter Lexi had been seducing Mitch instead.

"He was in love with Kate," Mitch said, which seemed to carry little or no weight.

The senator just glared and said, "I don't think we have anything left to discuss, Mr. Brody."

Mitch had never had to grovel in his life, but there was a first time for everything. His brother had damn well better appreciate this. "I'd like you to consider a compromise, sir."

The senator narrowed his eyes. "What kind of compromise?"

"We still need your support, Senator Cavanaugh, and I'm assuming you still want the best for your daughter."

"Your point is?"

"The Brody name can provide that."

"What are you suggesting?"

He had to force the words out. "A marriage between Alexis and me."

He looked wary, but also intrigued, leaning back in his seat and folding his arms over his chest. "Explain."

In other words, kiss the old man's ass, make this worth his while. "I think this arrangement will be in everyone's best interests, Senator. Married to me, Alexis will be set for life financially, and remain in the upper echelon of Texas society."

"And in return?" the senator asked.

"With your senatorial support, my brother and I will expand Brody Oil and Gas and take it to heights our father never dreamed possible."

"I'm sure you can imagine how humiliated my Lexi was when your first arrangement fell through. If I do say yes, what assurances do I have that you won't fall in love with *your* secretary and decide to marry her, instead?"

It annoyed Mitch the way he referred to her as "my Lexi," as though she were a possession, or a commodity. If he really cared about his daughter, would he expect her to settle for an arranged, loveless marriage? Wouldn't he want her to be happy? Or maybe in his mind, wealth and security equaled happiness.

Whatever the man's motivation, it wasn't Mitch's

problem. Besides, as far as he was concerned, Lexi was getting exactly what she deserved. He should have realized that the woman under the sweet and demure exterior was in reality a viper. Not unlike his mother, who made his father fall in love with her, gave birth to his sons and then abandoned them.

Lexi had played with his emotions and used him. Now he was going to return the favor.

"In the first place," Mitch told him, "my secretary is sixty-eight and married with grandchildren. Second, I am not a frivolous man when it comes to my emotions. I'm prepared to do anything for the sake of my business. I also have a plan to counteract any humiliation my brother's rejection caused. When all is said and done, Lance will be the one who comes out looking like a fool."

"How will you manage that?"

"With all due respect, sir, I would prefer to discuss it with Lexi first, to be sure that she's okay with it."

Senator Cavanaugh silently considered that for several moments, then he nodded. "I'm inclined to say yes, but under one condition. I won't force Lexi to marry you. She must be agreeable to the match, or the deal is off."

Mitch winced. That could definitely be a problem. She obviously despised Mitch. He was going to have to get creative, make her an offer she couldn't refuse. Perhaps a credit card with no limit and all the department store accounts she could dream of. He would give her everything her spoiled and greedy little heart desired. That is, if she *had* a heart.

"Agreed," Mitch said. He rose from his chair and offered the senator his hand. The man's grip was firm and binding.

"One more thing," the senator said, as Mitch turned to leave. "If you hurt my daughter in any way, shape or form, I will crush you and your brother. Understand?"

Mitch nodded, then turned and walked to the door, hoping he hadn't just made the biggest mistake of his life.

Lexi stood in her private bathroom at her father's Houston estate feeling as though she might be sick. She'd been feeling that way every morning lately. Which was what had motivated her to finally take a home pregnancy test. That, and two missed periods. And sure enough, when the little wand was ripe, up popped that little pink plus sign.

She groaned, and dropped her head in her hands. She had always been the perfect, dutiful daughter. The *one* time in her life she'd had the guts to say to hell with what her father wanted and have some fun, this was what happened.

Didn't that just figure?

There was a soft rap on the door and her personal assistant, Tara—the one who had been kind enough to fetch the pregnancy test in the first place—poked her head in. "Well?"

Unable to make herself say the words, Lexi held the results up so Tara could see for herself. "I am so completely screwed."

Tara crossed the room and wrapped Lexi up in a hug. "We'll get through this," she promised. "Everything will be okay."

Lexi rested her head on Tara's shoulder and let herself be comforted for a minute. Tara was the closest thing she had to a best friend. Lexi's father was particular about who Lexi was allowed to befriend. As far as he was concerned, no one was good enough for his little girl. As a result, people believed she was a snob.

And what would they think if she had a baby out of wedlock? Her father would be absolutely mortified. He talked for years about how someday she would marry and give him grandsons to spoil, but this was not part of his carefully laid plan.

"If my father finds out, he'll kill me," she said.

Tara held her at arm's length. "You have options."

Lexi knew exactly what she meant, and shook her head. "Termination isn't an option."

"So, you'll have it?"

"If I do, my father will disown me." Of that she had little doubt. Perception meant everything to him. He would probably accuse her of doing it on purpose, to sabotage his reputation. He would accuse her of not loving or respecting him after everything he had done for her. How many times had she been tempted to ask, *what have you done for me?* Other than shelter her, control her life and treat her more like political leverage than a daughter.

But she would never have the courage to say the words. Despite everything, he was still her father. Without him, she had no one.

"What do *you* want, Lexi?" Tara asked.

That was part of the problem. She didn't know what she wanted. If her father did disown her, cut her off financially, would it be fair to the child to raise it in poverty and shame? But the idea of a stranger raising her own flesh and blood made her heart ache.

This is Mitch's child, too, she reminded herself. Shouldn't he be part of the decision?

As if reading her mind, Tara asked, "What about the father?"

He may have been the biological father, but Mitch had made his feelings unequivocally clear. Their night together had been a mistake, and no one could ever know. "The father wants nothing to do with me."

"Curious," Tara said, looking thoughtful. "Mitchell Brody always struck me as the responsible type."

Lexi's mouth dropped open in surprise. She hadn't told anyone about the night she'd spent with her former fiancé's brother. It would have been too humiliating. How did Tara...?

"I would have to be an imbecile not to have figured it out," Tara told her. "For a week, you talked of nothing else. It was Mitch this and Mitch that. Mitch took me to the Smithsonian and Mitch took me to the most exclusive French restaurant in all of D.C. Mitch and I sat talking for hours. It was obvious you had feelings for him. A woman doesn't hold on to her virginity for twenty-four years, then give it up to a stranger."

That week had been one of the best in her life. She had learned that there was more to Mitch than his serious, and sometimes intimidating exterior. He could be sweet and fun. She'd allowed him to seduce her, and look at the mess it had gotten her into.

"On the other hand," Tara said, "if he was really *that* responsible, he would have used protection."

"He did! That's why I was so hesitant to believe I could be pregnant in the first place."

"Did you use a condom *every* time?"

"Of course we—" She frowned.

Tara mirrored her expression. "What?"

Lexi shook her head. "No, that couldn't be it."

"You had unprotected sex?"

"Only for a minute. It was the middle of the night, and we woke up and he started to…" Her cheeks blushed a brilliant shade of pink. She'd never spoken about anything so personal to anyone in her life. Not even her physician. "But he put a condom on before he…you know…finished."

Tara looked pained. "Sperm can be released before ejaculation. And it only takes one. They teach this stuff in health class, Lex."

But she hadn't had health class. She had been homeschooled by tutors, to spare her the improper influence of other children. And not a single one of those tutors, not even her science instructor, had ever said a word about sex education. Her father would have had a fit. Everything she knew about sex, she'd learned from the romance novels she used to sneak into the house. Lately, she had come to realize that those books offered a somewhat slanted view of what love and relationships truly entailed.

"So, this is my fault," she said. If she hadn't been so naive, she would have known better.

"It's no one's fault. Besides, it sounds like you two had one heck of a night together. Maybe, if there's a chance—"

Lexi shook her head. "There's no chance. He wasn't the man I thought he was."

"Well, he still has rights."

"I know," she said, feeling more confused than she ever had in her life. "I don't know what to do."

"Maybe what you need is some time away to think this through. You've been telling me for months that you'd like to take a vacation. Didn't you mention a trip to Cabo San Lucas?"

The place where she had hoped to spend her honeymoon in marital bliss with Mitch? She couldn't bear the thought of it.

"Too hot," she told Tara.

"Okay, how about an Alaskan cruise?"

She blanched. "As if I'm not nauseous enough."

"I didn't think about that." Tara gnawed her lower lip for a moment, then she brightened. "I know! What about that villa in the Greek Isles that Senator Richardson mentioned? That would be perfect."

Actually, that was an excellent idea. She wanted quiet and seclusion, and no one in Greece was likely to know, or even care, who her father happened to be. But there was still a problem. "What if my father won't allow it?"

"Tell him the humiliation of Lance's rejection is just too much to bear, and you need some time alone."

It was the humiliation of Mitch's rejection that was really killing her, but still, it wasn't a bad idea.

"Make him feel guilty for putting you in this position," Tara said. "It is ultimately his fault that you're going through all this."

Tara had a point. If her father hadn't insisted she marry Lance, Lexi never would have met Mitch. So, in a roundabout way he was responsible, although she doubted he would agree. He would lay the blame solely on her. As always. No matter how hard she tried, she never seemed to do anything right. And though she had never been one to play the pity card, if the circumstance demanded it…

She smiled at her friend, thankful she had someone so supportive to lean on at a time like this, even if she was getting paid handsomely to do so. "How soon can you make the reservation?"

Three

As soon as he left the senator's office, Mitch called his brother.

Lance answered on the first ring. "What did he say?"

"He agreed."

Lance released a breath.

"You're sure you're ready to deal with the backlash?" Mitch asked. "This isn't going to look great for you."

"After the way I humiliated her, I would say I probably deserve it. I'm just sorry that you have to go through this."

"Sorry for what? You were going to make the same sacrifice."

"But I didn't. I went with my heart."

"I'm sure Lexi and I will eventually grow fond of one another," he lied. It was probably more likely they would live completely separate lives. If they didn't kill each other first.

"I just feel guilty as hell making you do this. Now that I know what it feels like to be with someone I love and trust, I want the same for you. I want you to be happy."

"When our company is thriving and we're leaving our competitors in the dust, I will be. Besides, you know I don't believe in love. Life doesn't work that way. Not for me, anyhow." Nor did he want it to. It was tough to betray a man who refused to leave himself vulnerable. No woman would hurt him the way his mother had.

His brother could see right through him. "Not all women abandon their families," he said. "And when Mom did, I'm sure she had her reasons."

Of course she did. Their father was a bastard, emotionally, and at times physically, abusive. But if she loved Mitch and Lance, why leave them behind to suffer in her place? Why not take them with her?

He had no doubt that Lexi was self-centered and spoiled enough to do the same. If she did agree to marry him, he would insist they remain childless. It would be cruel to bring a baby into a loveless shell of a marriage. Sometimes he wished his parents would have spared him the burden of ever being born.

"There is a catch," Mitch told him. "Alexis has to willingly accept my proposal."

Lance let out a low whistle. "Maybe it was my imagination, but there didn't seem to be any love lost between the two of you when I broke the engagement."

Lance had no idea. "He also warned me that if I hurt her, he'll crush us."

Lance chuckled. "The old goat doesn't pull any punches, does he?"

"You're not concerned?"

"Why should I be? I have total faith in you."

Mitch hoped that faith wasn't misplaced. He'd already let his brother down once, betraying him by sleeping with his soon-to-be fiancée. Although it wasn't as if Lance loved Lexi, or thought of the marriage as anything more than a business arrangement. Mitch, on the other hand, had honestly believed there had been a connection between Lexi and him. If he had known that Lance loved Kate the night that he slept with Lexi, he might have asked Lexi to marry him, instead. But she had only been using him.

Ironic that he would be stuck marrying her regardless.

"You can still back out," Lance said.

No, he couldn't. This marriage was imperative. "I've already made my decision. I'm going to call her right now and set up a meeting."

"Suppose you ask, and she says no."

A very likely scenario. But every woman had a weakness. He would find hers and use it to his advantage. "I'll just have to make her an offer she can't refuse."

Though she hadn't yet sought her father's approval, Lexi laid out her clothes for the maid to pack. Her plane departed the day after tomorrow and nothing short of the apocalypse would stop her from being on it. The way she figured it, an emotional meltdown during supper and tearful pleading should bend him to her will.

Her cell phone rang and she checked the display. It was a Houston number that she didn't recognize. Curious, she answered.

"Lexi, it's Mitchell Brody."

Her heart plummeted to her toes at the sound of his voice. "Hello, Mr. Brody," she said in her coolest tone.

"I was wondering if we can arrange a meeting. This afternoon, if possible."

A meeting? What could they possibly have to say to each other?

Fear slithered down her spine. He couldn't know about the baby, could he? Only Tara knew, and she swore not to breathe a word to anyone.

She was being paranoid. Of course he didn't know. Anything he could possibly have to say to her at this point was irrelevant.

"I'm afraid I don't have time," she told him. "I'm packing for a trip. Perhaps we could schedule a meeting in a few weeks, after I return." Maybe by then she would know what she planned to do.

"I'm afraid this can't wait," he said. "It's urgent that I speak with you today. I can be there in twenty minutes."

Though he was the last man on earth that she wanted to see right now, her curiosity had been piqued. Maybe he wanted to beg her forgiveness, tell her that calling their night together a mistake had been a gross error in judgment.

Maybe he was coming to tell her that he loved her. She could at least hear him out, let him grovel a little before she told him to go to hell.

"Fine," she said.

"I'll see you in twenty minutes."

Mitch was at her door in fifteen. When the bell rang, she waved the butler away and answered it herself.

She'd almost forgotten how beautiful he was, how tall and dark and imposing. How delicious he smelled. Some small part of her ached to be close to him, to touch him again, to vault herself into his arms. Probably thanks to the pregnancy hormones that had been wreaking havoc with her emotions the past few weeks.

The easy smile Mitch usually wore was absent. His jaw was set and his expression serious. In fact, he looked almost…nervous. She didn't think men like Mitch ever got nervous.

"Thank you for agreeing to see me," he said.

She folded her arms across her chest. "What was so important that it couldn't wait?"

"Is there somewhere we can speak privately?"

She nodded, and he followed her across the foyer to the study. When they were inside, she shut the door. "Well?"

"First, I want to apologize again for my brother's behavior."

"Don't bother. He did me a favor. We would have been miserable together." She paused, then asked, "How is Lance?"

"Great. Very happy."

"I'm glad. But that isn't what you came here to talk about."

"No, it isn't," he said, looking troubled. "As you probably know, Lance and I are still in need of your father's support."

"Good luck with that." Her father had been furious with the Brody brothers, and still was, as far as she could tell.

"I had a meeting with him today."

Her eyes widened. "He actually agreed to meet with you?"

"I can be very persuasive."

He didn't have to tell her that. Had he not been so persuasive, she wouldn't be in her current dilemma.

"The senator and I have reached an…understanding."

Why did she get the feeling that she wasn't going to like this?

"What kind of understanding?"

"Your father has promised his support if you marry me, instead."

Marry him? After what had happened with Lance, would her father honestly force her to marry the other Brody brother? And why hadn't he said anything to her? Why hadn't he warned her?

"Another business arrangement?" she asked, and Mitch nodded. "Do I have a choice in the matter?"

"In fact, you do. The stipulation was that I have to convince you to marry me."

Her mouth fell open. "He actually *said* that?"

"Essentially, yes."

She could see that the prospect of having to beg Lexi to marry him made Mitch uncomfortable. As it should, after the way he'd used her. Score one for good ol' Dad. And she knew exactly why the senator had agreed to this arrangement. He'd mentioned more than once that he believed Mitch possessed presidential-size political potential. Social status meant everything to him and he would love nothing more than to see his precious daughter serve as first lady to the nation.

Whether or not Mitch was the least bit interested in a political career, Lexi didn't have a clue, and the idea of spending the rest of her life married to someone so coldhearted and manipulative—too much like her father—turned her already questionable stomach.

Yet she couldn't deny that this could be the answer to all of her problems. Marrying Mitch would give her child legitimacy. Although people—her father in particular—might get suspicious when she gave birth to a full-term-size baby two months early. But she could figure that out later.

The real question was, could she stand to be married to Mitch for the rest of her life?

Even if she did decide to marry him, she wouldn't let Mitch off the hook too easily. She was going to make him work for it.

"After the way your brother humiliated me, what makes you believe I would even consider marrying you?" she asked.

"Because I have a plan that will leave my brother looking like the humiliated one."

She narrowed her eyes at him, unable to resist taking the bait. "How will you manage that?"

"It will be leaked that you and I have been secretly seeing each other, and that I seduced you away from my brother that week in D.C. People will be led to believe that you were planning to break the engagement, only Lance did it first, before you had the chance."

"And what will make them believe that? What if they think it's just gossip?"

"My brother and I will have a very public argument to drive the point home."

Reputation was everything to men like Lance and

Mitch, so she couldn't help but feel the slightest bit touched. "Lance would do that for me?"

"We'll do anything for the sake of our business."

So, they weren't doing this for her. They were doing it for their business. Her vindication was just a convenient side effect. She should have known.

Ironically, their so-called plan wasn't that far from the truth. Mitch *had* seduced her, and for a short time she had seriously considered choosing him over his brother.

"Does Lance know what happened?" she asked.

"You mean that night at the hotel?"

She nodded.

"Of course not. As far as he's concerned, this is a total fabrication."

And she could see from Mitch's demeanor that he intended to keep it that way. That would be tough when news of the baby broke. Lance was eventually going to find out.

The truth was, she cared little about her humiliation, and what people might think of her. For the baby's sake, however, she would be a fool to turn down Mitch's offer. A marriage to him would grant the kind of life that the baby deserved.

"My answer is yes," she said. "I'll marry you."

He looked surprised that she would acquiesce so easily. "We should do it soon. I was thinking a small civil ceremony at the courthouse."

The sooner—and the simpler—the better as far

as she was concerned. So much for the extravagant and blissful white wedding she had always dreamed of. "Fine."

"And we should plan a honeymoon. To make it look more authentic."

She thought of the nonrefundable trip she had just booked. "I'm leaving for a seven-day trip to Greece the day after tomorrow. Would that be authentic enough for you?"

He nodded. "That would be perfect."

"I'll have my assistant book you a seat."

"And I'll have mine make the wedding arrangements."

"All right."

"While we're away, I'll arrange to have your things moved into my townhouse."

She hadn't given any thought to the fact that he would expect her to live with him. But of course he would. Married couples lived together. Although the idea of living under his roof made her feel vulnerable. Would he try to run her life, controlling her every move the way her father had? Would she be moving from one prison to another?

And if so, what choice did she have?

Mitch must have read her expression. "You'll have your own room," he assured her. "You'll want for nothing."

Unfortunately, that wasn't true. She wanted something he wasn't capable of giving. She wanted to be loved. She wanted someone to respect and appreciate her for who she was deep down inside. And while he did seem to appreciate what she was doing for him, the love and respect part seemed impossible. Maybe she wasn't worthy. Maybe that was the price she paid for wealth and security. Or maybe the sad truth was, she just wasn't all that lovable.

"You won't regret this," Mitch assured her, which she found terribly ironic, seeing as how she was beginning to regret it already.

"Are you ready for this?" Lance asked Mitch the following evening. They sat across from one another at a linen-draped table in the elaborately decorated dining room of the Texas Cattleman's Club. It was the most public place they could think of for the desired result. If all went as planned, word of what was about to transpire would burn up the town like flaming tumbleweed in the dry season.

"I'm ready," Mitch said.

It was a little hard to believe that this time tomorrow he would be married and on his way to Greece. Twenty-nine was too damned young to be a husband, to be tied down. Not that he or Lexi were thinking of this as a real marriage. It was a business arrangement. One that would no doubt cost him dearly. Both emotionally and financially. That was evident from the astronomically priced wedding ring she'd chosen. Her expensive taste apparently knew no bounds.

A grin kicked up one corner of Lance's mouth. "I'll go easy on you, little brother."

"Don't bother. Whatever you can dish out, I can take." God knows that there were many times he'd gotten a lot worse from their old man. "We have to make this look real, Lance."

"Don't worry, I will," he said, and just like that, the grin faded. Lance assumed a look of pure disgust, and said in a voice loud enough for the entire room to hear, "You son of a bitch."

A hush fell over the room and all heads turned in their direction. No turning back now, Mitch thought.

He held up both hands in a defensive gesture and said in a pleading voice, "Let me explain."

Lance stood so fast his chair flipped backward onto the floor, narrowly missing the table behind theirs. He grabbed his half-full highball glass, rose to his feet and with a flick of his wrist flung the contents into Mitch's face. As the alcohol burned Mitch's eyes and soaked through the front of his shirt, he couldn't help but think, *what a terrible waste of the club's finest whiskey.*

Gasps of surprise filled the silence as Lance stormed from the dining room. Mitch grabbed a linen napkin from the table and wiped his face. With all eyes on him now—most of them friends, neighbors or business associates—he jumped up from his chair and followed his brother to the crowded main lobby, calling, "Lance, wait! I can explain!"

He caught up with him just outside the dining room door. To anyone watching, Lance appeared enraged. "*Explain?* What sort of man seduces his brother's fiancée?"

Mitch heard gasps from the crowd.

"We didn't mean for it to happen," he said, finding it ironic that if Lance had discovered the truth, Mitch probably would have been saying the same thing. Although it would have been a lie. Lexi had admitted to using him to rob her husband of her virginity. Seems the joke was on both of them.

"As far as I'm concerned, you and Lexi deserve each other," Lance spat, and turned to leave. Just as they had choreographed, Mitch grabbed his arm.

The fist came at him so swiftly that, had he not expected it, he wouldn't have had time to duck. As it was, Mitch could only stand there defenseless as Lance's fist connected squarely with his jaw. The blow knocked him backward several feet. He lost his balance and ended up on his ass on the unforgiving marble floor.

Lance shot him one last seething look, then shouldered his way out the door. Mitch's behind ached something special, his jaw stung like a mother and his pride had taken a hit, but the reaction from the patrons told him it had all been worth it. A steady buzz of voices hummed through the lobby and at least half a dozen people were jabbering excitedly into their cell phones. He gave it an hour before the entire population of Maverick County heard the news.

Mitch swiped a hand across the corner of his mouth and came back with a smear of blood. Two employees appeared at either side to help him to his feet, and the hostess handed him a napkin to stop the bleeding.

"I'm all right," he mumbled, shrugging away from their help as though humiliated and distraught. From outside, he heard the squeal of tires and knew Lance was peeling out of the lot, putting the finishing touches on their little charade. And what a show it had been.

He just hoped it was worth it.

Four

With only Tara, Lance, and Mitch's best friend Justin Dupree to serve as witnesses—her father had been called to D.C. on so-called urgent business—Lexi and Mitch said their "I do's" before a county judge the following morning, then drove directly to the airport to catch the first leg of their flight to Greece.

Lexi sat beside her new husband in first class, eyes closed, willing her stomach to settle. Either her hormones were wreaking havoc on her nerves, or her morning sickness had taken a severe turn for the worse. If it was the latter, to hell with having three or four children. This kid could count on being an only child. Up until now, she'd suffered only occasional, mild nausea. Today, she had vomited three times. Once at home, right after she crawled out of bed, once in the ladies' room of the courthouse, and again in the airport bathroom just before their flight boarded. She was beginning to think this trip was a bad idea.

Even worse than marrying Mitch Brody.

"Are you all right?" Mitch said softly.

Far from it. She swallowed back the bile rising in her throat and opened her eyes, grimacing once again when she saw the angry-looking bruise that spanned the left side of his jaw and the nasty gash at the corner of his mouth.

"I'm fine," she lied.

There was concern etched on his face. He folded the newspaper he'd been reading—the financial section, of course—and set it in his lap. "No offense, but you're looking a little green."

How nice of him to notice. "And you're looking black and blue."

He reached up and rubbed a palm across his jaw, wincing slightly.

"I can't believe he hit you. Couldn't he just have pretended to punch you?"

Mitch shrugged, as if it was no big deal. "I told you, it had to look convincing."

Apparently it had. According to Tara, the entire town was buzzing with gossip, and every chance Tara got, she helped out by fanning the flames. In no time, everyone would be convinced that Mitch and Lexi had been having a secret affair. News of the baby would only cement the rumors.

Even though Lexi knew Mitch and Lance had ultimately done it for their business, she couldn't help but feel honored that they had gone to such lengths in part to salvage her honor.

And she thought chivalry was dead.

Despite his casual attitude, it must have been humiliating for Mitch. Or maybe he was one of those men who honestly didn't give a damn what anyone thought.

"I could ring the flight attendant for an ice pack," she offered.

"I'm fine," he said. "Do you need anything?"

She shook her head, which was a mistake because the movement made her stomach lurch. She wished she'd chosen a more casual outfit for the flight instead of the fitted silk suit she'd worn for the ceremony. Something loose and comfortable, like her pajamas.

"You don't look well," he said.

"Thanks."

"That wasn't an insult. I'm concerned."

"I'm just a little airsick. It happens sometimes. And it's kind of embarrassing, so if you don't mind, can we just drop it?"

"Sorry."

After that, they sat in awkward silence. During

their week together in D.C. they had seemingly endless conversations. Most people viewed her as a spoiled and witless debutante, and her father didn't help, perpetuating the rumors by pampering and coddling her. But Mitch had seen past that. He had listened to her, made her feel…special. Now she had no idea what to say to him.

How about something along the lines of, *By the way, did I mention that I'm pregnant with your child?*

She had planned to tell him in the limo on the way to the airport, but she'd been otherwise occupied, trying not to be sick all over the leather interior. She'd decided to wait until they settled into the villa in Greece. She didn't doubt the news was going to come as a shock, but she was sure that when he grew used to the idea, he would be happy to be a father.

As if reading her thoughts, Mitch said, "Maybe we should have a talk about our expectations in regard to our relationship."

She hoped he wasn't talking about sex, because that hadn't been part of the deal. This was supposed to be a business arrangement. She had no intention of being his concubine. "What kind of expectations?"

Her wariness seemed to amuse him. "Not the kind you're obviously thinking of. Our relationship stops at the bedroom door."

"Good," she said, feeling relieved. And strangely enough, a little disappointed.

"What I meant, for example, is that as a part of my business, it's required that I occasionally attend social functions. As my wife, I will expect you to accompany me, and of course I'll do the same for you."

That didn't sound so terrible. "I can do that."

"You'll also be expected to host several parties."

That was something that she was actually quite good at. "Of course."

"And since I'm not particularly fond of seeing my name in the tabloids, or being the source of the latest gossip, I think it should appear to everyone that we're happily married. If word gets out that this is part of a business deal, we'll never hear the end of it. I personally value my privacy."

Personally, she didn't give a damn what people thought. But for the baby's sake, it would be best if they kept up a ruse of wedded bliss, so the child wouldn't feel unwanted.

"As soon as we get back to the states we can start house hunting. Or if you prefer, we could build."

"What about your townhouse?"

"It's too small for our needs."

"If you think so," she said. She had never actually been there, but she couldn't imagine that someone as wealthy as Mitch would live anywhere that could be considered small. Although she couldn't deny that the idea of having her own home was a little exciting. All of her life she had lived in her father's Houston estate or D.C. townhouse. He hadn't even allowed her to decorate her own room, preferring instead to let a professional choose the decor. She had never had a place that was truly hers.

"Of course, you'll be in charge of the household," Mitch continued. "You'll be responsible for the hiring and dismissal of the staff."

"Will I be allowed to decorate?" she asked.

The question seemed to puzzle him. "Of course."

"I won't need your approval for every little thing I do?"

He looked confused. "Is there a reason you should?"

She had just assumed that, like her father, Mitch would deem her untrustworthy or incapable. Or maybe he was just saying these things to lull her into a false sense of security. Maybe he would be an overbearing tyrant.

And maybe you're paranoid.

"Other than the obvious financial requirements, is there anything specific that you expect from me?"

She wasn't sure what he meant by financial requirements. Did he think she would expect him to pay her a salary? "What 'financial requirements' are we talking about?"

"Credit cards, cash. As I assured you, you won't want for anything."

Despite what most people believed, she wasn't the spoiled, pampered heiress they described in the society pages of the paper. Her father had always provided her with a generous allowance for clothing and essentials, but otherwise kept her on a pretty short fiscal leash. He monitored her credit card statements to be sure that she wasn't spending his money on anything inappropriate, and he limited the amount of cash she was allowed. She'd always wondered what it would feel like to be financially independent, to not have someone scrutinizing her every move.

If Mitch did give her financial freedom, maybe this marriage deal wouldn't be quite as miserable as she'd expected.

"Come on," he said. "There must be *something* you want."

Though she was going to wait, he'd left the subject wide open, and she couldn't resist dipping her toes in to test the waters. "What about children?"

"What about them?"

"Well, I know this is just a business arrangement, but I've always wanted kids."

The dark expression that spread across his face chilled her to her core. He shook his head and said, "I think that would be a bad idea."

Oh, this was not good.

Maybe it was the act of conceiving the baby that he had a problem with. Maybe he no longer found her attractive. Their kiss after the vows couldn't have been colder or more formal. Maybe she had been so terrible in bed that first time, he had no interest in a repeat performance.

"If it's the intimacy you're concerned about," she said, "there are other ways—"

"It has nothing to do with that. I feel it would be unfair to bring a child into a loveless marriage."

Her stomach bottomed out. How would he feel if he didn't have a choice in the matter? Would he insist on a divorce? Tell her father the truth about what happened in D.C.? Or even worse, would he disown his child? Then where would she be?

A sense of panic filled her. There had to be a way to convince him, to make this right. "Maybe if we—"

"No," he said firmly, his mouth set in a stubborn line. "There is no maybe. I'll give you anything you want, Lexi. Anything but this."

Just because they didn't love each other, it didn't have to mean their child wouldn't be happy. Her mind worked frantically on a way to make him change his mind.

What if she did everything he asked of her and became the perfect wife? Then would he accept the idea of having a child? But is that what she really wanted? To live a lie?

At this point, did she even have a choice?

Mitch felt slightly guilty for denying Lexi something she obviously longed for, but she would just have to get used to not getting everything her greedy little heart desired. He was sure that no matter how much she thought she wanted children, she had no idea what kind of responsibility it would be. He knew from experience that spoiled debutantes like her didn't have time for anyone but themselves. She would grow tired of the burden, just as his mother had, and walk away. He refused to allow his child to grow up unable to count on the one person who was supposed to provide unconditional love.

They endured the remainder of the nine-hour flight engaged in occasional strained small talk, with Mitch always initiating the conversation. The way she had talked nonstop in D.C., he could only assume that she was now giving him the silent treatment. She probably wasn't accustomed to people not catering to her every whim.

Well, she would have to get used to it. He didn't intend to deny her happiness, but he wasn't about to pamper or spoil her, either. It was time she began living in the real world.

After a brief layover in London, which Lexi spent the majority of in the ladies' room, they boarded a flight for Athens. Lexi fell asleep the minute the wheels left the tarmac and didn't wake until they landed. A limo met them outside the airport to bring them to the port of Lavrio where they boarded the small passenger ship that would take them to the island of Tzia.

Two hours later, and sixteen hours after they left Houston, they finally arrived at the villa where they would spend the next week. About half a mile east, he could see rows of densely built houses that looked like windowed shoe boxes clinging to the steep slope that bordered the village of Loulida, and nothing but open countryside for at least half a mile in every other direction. When Lexi said the area was secluded, he hadn't realized just how alone they would be.

Mitch let Lexi have the top-level master suite and took one of the three guest bedrooms on the ground floor for himself. It was more than enough space for him, and a large sliding glass door conveniently led to the swimming pool, hot tub and pool house, where he guessed he would be spending much of his time. Just off the bedrooms was a spacious living room with a full bar and plush, comfortable-looking furniture. The middle floor held a modern and well-equipped kitchen with an adjoining dining room, while another comfortable sitting room led to the main terrace and the barbecue area.

The interior was a combination of vibrant colors and innovative designs that could have very comfortably housed half a dozen people or more. His preference would have been a place that was smaller, and more intimate. But someone like Lexi would want the biggest and most luxurious lodging available. Although he was a bit surprised that she hadn't hired a full staff to cater to her. She hadn't even arranged for a chef or a maid.

"I think I'll lie down for a while," she said, when he carried her luggage to her room for her. She was still looking a little green, and he couldn't help feeling sorry for her. He had never been one to suffer from motion sickness, but from the looks of it, the last day had been hell.

"Can I bring you anything?" he asked. "Something to eat? A cup of tea?"

"I think I just need to sleep for a while," she said, but looked at him a little funny, as though she couldn't figure out why he was being so nice to her.

That makes two of us, sweetheart. Must be jet lag, or temporary insanity.

"I'll be in my room unpacking if you need me," he told her, then he left her room, closing the door behind him. Something seemed different. Lexi was acting almost…humbled.

He shook his head. It was probably just due to the fact that she was feeling sick. He was sure she would be back to her entitled, narcissistic self by tomorrow.

As he walked to his room he pulled out his cell and dialed his brother, and though it was barely 7:00 a.m. in Texas, he answered on the first ring.

"You're supposed to be on your honeymoon," Lance said.

"I am."

"Then why the hell are you calling me?"

"I just wondered if there's anything new from Darius about the fire. Anything pointing to Alex Montoya."

"Nothing since you left, which was less than

twenty-four hours ago. And if I do hear something, I'll let you know."

In other words, don't call me, I'll call you. "If there are any problems at the office—"

"Mitch, forget about work and enjoy yourself. You're on your honeymoon. Go seduce your wife or something."

"You know as well as I do that it isn't that kind of marriage."

"You're a newlywed, and the way I look at it, that gives you certain rights. Like sex with your new wife on your wedding night. I guarantee you won't be disappointed."

Mitch knew that firsthand, but the question was, how did Lance? Then he realized: Lance must have slept with her when they were engaged.

Lexi certainly hadn't wasted any time hopping from one brother's bed to the next, he thought wryly. Maybe to her, it was just a game. Some kind of twisted challenge. At least Mitch knew for a fact that he had been first. And according to Lexi, that was exactly the way she'd planned it. What she hadn't counted on was Lance dumping her for someone else.

"I felt kind of sorry for her yesterday," Lance said.

"Why?"

"Having only her assistant at her wedding. You would think her father would have the decency to show."

"He's a busy man."

"Too busy to see his only child get married? Would you miss your daughter's wedding?"

No, but then, he wouldn't be having a daughter, or a son. He would just have to be content spoiling the children that he was sure Lance and Kate would have. "I'm sure the senator had his reasons."

"That doesn't make it any less lousy."

Mitch couldn't help thinking she got exactly what she deserved.

After he hung up with his brother, Mitch took a long, hot shower to wash away the travel grit, then collapsed naked between the cool silk sheets. He decided he would sleep for an hour or so, then get up and make them something to eat. But when he opened his eyes again the sun had already set, and the room was dark but for the light in the hallway shining through the open door.

Hadn't he closed the door before he'd lain down? He was almost positive he had. In fact, he *was* positive.

Then he saw a silhouette move across the room. He jerked up on his elbows, groggy and alarmed, but as his eyes adjusted, he realized the form was female. And not just any female.

It was Lexi.

Five

Lexi crossed the room to Mitch's bed wearing a floor-length, low-cut, white silk nightgown that shimmered in the light. Her pale hair lay in soft waves across her shoulders, cascading down to the swell of her breasts.

For a second he wondered if he was dreaming. What reason would she possibly have to be in his room? Was she sick? Or plotting to smother him with his pillow?

"Is something wrong?" he asked, his voice rough from sleep.

"Nothing is wrong."

Relieved, he dropped his head back down on the bed. "What are you doing in here?"

"This is officially our wedding night," she said.

Yeah, so? he thought, unsure of the significance. Then she lifted the gown up over her head and dropped it to the floor. She wasn't wearing anything underneath. Now he knew he *had* to be dreaming. But as she slipped between the sheets beside him, her body warm and soft against his, it was too vivid, too fantastic to be anything but real. Nothing about this made any sense.

"This wasn't part of the deal," he reminded her.

She leaned on one elbow, gazing down at him. In the dim light she looked like an angel, when he knew for a fact she was actually a devil in disguise. "I know."

She laid her hand on his chest, lightly stroking his skin, and his body responded instantly. She was obviously willing, so why couldn't he shake the feeling that something wasn't right? Why did he feel guilty, as though he was forcing her?

"We don't have to," he said, even though he wanted nothing more than to run his fingers through the silky ribbons of her hair and pull her down for a long, deep kiss. He didn't want her to feel as though she owed him, or was somehow obligated.

Uncertainty flickered in her eyes, and in that instant he had never seen a woman look more vulnerable or insecure. Deep inside of him something hard and unyielding softened a bit around the edges. Was it possible that she wasn't as confident and fearless as she liked people to believe?

She pulled her hand away and said, "We won't if you don't want to."

Was she serious? He couldn't think of a single other thing he would rather be doing. He took her by the wrist and guided her hand under the covers to his erection. "Does it feel like I don't want to?"

A smile crept across her face as she wrapped her hand around him and squeezed. The sensation was so erotic he nearly lost it.

"I want you, Mitch," she whispered.

That was all the convincing he needed. He caught her behind the neck, pulled her to him and kissed her.

One second Lexi was lying across Mitch's chest as he tangled his fingers through her hair and ravaged her mouth, and the next she was flat on her back on the bed looking up at him. The change of position was so swift it left her breathless and dizzy. Or maybe it was his kisses that were doing that. She just prayed, as he pressed his weight against her, caressing her skin with his hands and his mouth, that he didn't feel her trembling. She didn't want him to know how terrified she had been that he might reject her. She had no clue how to play the role of vixen, how to be the aggressor, but if she was going to convince him this was a real marriage, if she was going to make him fall in love with her, she had to play the part. What kind of wife would she be if she didn't please her husband sexually? Especially on their wedding night.

Although right now, he seemed to be the one doing all the pleasing, and she had almost forgotten how impossibly wonderful it felt to be close to him. How he made her feel as though she was the most beautiful, desirable woman in the world.

"I thought we were keeping this relationship outside the bedroom," he said, nibbling his way down her throat. On the contrary, it was her intention to keep him in bed as much as humanly possible while they were in Greece.

"Not that I'm complaining," he added. "Just mildly confused."

"We both have needs," she said. "I figure, if we have to be stuck with each other, why not enjoy it?"

He grinned down at her. "Lexi, isn't that supposed to be *my* line?"

"You know what I think?" she asked, and his brow perked with curiosity. "I think you talk too much."

His grin turned feral. "And I like the way you think."

She wrapped her arms around his neck and pulled him to her for a slow, deep kiss. They caressed and touched each other until she felt as though she would go out of her mind. She wanted him inside her so badly, she actually ached.

"Make love to me," she told him. "Right now."

Mitch looked up from the nipple he'd been teasing with his tongue. "I thought that's what I was doing."

"Maybe you could do it a little faster?"

"What's the hurry?"

All she knew was that it felt as though there was a big empty space inside of her that she was desperate to fill. He must have seen the desperation on her face because he opened the drawer on the bedside table and pulled out a condom. At her questioning look he said, "Doesn't hurt to come prepared."

She didn't tell him there was no point, that the damage was already done.

He rolled it on, then entered her with one slow but purposeful thrust. She gasped at the stinging sensation as her body stretched to accept him.

Concern filled his eyes. "Did I hurt you?"

"No," she lied, because it was a good hurt. Since that night at the hotel, she'd had the constant and nagging feeling that something was missing. She had felt…incomplete. Now, with their bodies joined, she finally felt whole again.

She arched up, taking him even deeper inside of her, wrapping her legs around his waist. Mitch groaned and grasped the bedcovers. It gave her a thrilling sense of power to know that he was losing control, and she was making it happen.

He rolled over so that she was on top, straddling him, their bodies still joined. Now that she was up here, she was unsure of what to do. What if she did it wrong and made a fool of herself? What if she was clumsy and awkward, and couldn't satisfy him? "Mitch, I don't—"

"Yes, you do," he said, as though he had complete confidence in her. "Just do what feels good."

She braced her hands on the mattress on either side of him and rose up, but she went too far and he slipped out. She made a noise of frustration, but Mitch didn't seem to mind.

"Don't worry," he said, guiding himself back in like it was no big deal. This time he rested his hands on her hips to guide her. "Take it slow."

She began to move slowly, eyes closed in concentration. At first, she was so afraid to make a mistake, focused so completely on her every move, she wasn't able to let herself enjoy it.

"Relax," he said, arching his hips up to meet her downward thrusts. They slipped into a slow, steady rhythm, and she began to lose herself in the sensation, in the sweet friction, until it began to feel as natural as breathing.

This was the way she wanted to spend the rest of her life. Acting on impulse, living by instinct. Doing things just because they felt good.

"Open your eyes," Mitch said, and when she did, when she looked down at him, she could see that he was barely hanging on.

With his eyes locked on hers, he reached down to where their bodies met and stroked her. Pleasure rippled through her from the inside out and an orgasm that was almost shocking in its intensity locked her muscles. She threw her head back and rode out the sensation, and through a haze she heard Mitch groan, felt him tense beneath her, his fingers digging into her skin.

Limp with satisfaction, Lexi collapsed against his chest, their hearts pounding out a frantic beat together. It just kept getting better and better. She had never felt as close to anyone in her life as she did to Mitch tonight.

This was going to work, she assured herself. Everything was going to be fine. But as he rolled her over and began kissing her, making love to her all over again, she couldn't help feeling like a fraud.

Mitch woke the next morning and reached for Lexi, but her side of the bed was empty. He glanced over at the clock, surprised to see that it was after eight. Jet lag had his schedule all jacked up, because he never slept a minute past 6:00 a.m., even on weekends. He sat up and looked groggily around the room, thinking that maybe Lexi had just stepped into the bathroom, but he could hear the clatter of pots and pans and dishes in the kitchen. He caught a whiff of something that smelled like breakfast, but he knew he must be imagining it, unless she had hired a cook after all.

He rolled out of bed, pulled on a pair of pajama bottoms and walked to the kitchen. Lexi stood by the stove, poking at something in a frying pan with a spatula. On the counter sat a plate with some sort of sausage.

She cooked?

Beside her, the state-of-the-art dishwasher was open and there were actually dishes inside. He didn't think a spoiled heiress even knew what a dishwasher was, much less knew how to use one.

Was it possible that he'd misjudged her?

"Good morning," he said.

She turned to him and smiled a sweet smile that made him believe she was genuinely happy to see him. "Good morning."

She was wearing the silk gown she'd had on last night and her feet were bare. Her hair was pulled back in a ponytail and her face was free of makeup. She looked young and sweet and pretty, but from the neck down, she was all woman. Full and firm breasts, perfectly proportioned hips. He had to fight the urge to scoop her up in his arms and carry her back to bed. Having a little occasional fun was one thing, but they shouldn't overdo it. He didn't want her getting the wrong idea.

"Are you hungry?" she asked. "I made breakfast."

"Starved," he said. They had skipped dinner last night. "Can I help?"

"I've got it. Do you want coffee?"

"I can get it," he said, but she shooed him away.

"Go sit down. Relax."

Ooookay.

He took a seat in the nook by a window overlooking the pool, while she filled a cup that was already sitting by the coffeemaker.

"Milk or sugar?" she asked.

"Black, please."

She laughed lightly and shook her head.

"What?" he asked.

"It's just weird," she said, crossing the room and setting the cup in front of him. "We're married and I don't even know how you take your coffee. I guess this just wasn't the way I imagined my life."

Amen to that. He never imagined himself ever getting married. He would have been happy playing the field the rest of his life. Having relationships on his terms. Living life by his own rules.

She walked back to the stove and he was mesmerized watching her hips sway, the curve of her behind under the silk gown. He couldn't help but wonder if she was commando under there. If so, it wouldn't take much to lift up the gown and pull her into his lap....

He gave his head a shake. He needed to stop with the fantasies and keep his hands to himself.

She scooped scrambled eggs onto his plate, added a few links of sausage and then set the plate in front of him. *"Bon appétit,"* she said, then sat down across from him and rested her chin on her clasped hands.

"Aren't you eating?" he asked.

She shook her head. "I had something when I got up."

He stabbed a forkful of eggs and shoveled it into his mouth...and nearly spit it back out. The eggs were so salty he almost gagged. He forced himself to swallow and chased it down with a guzzle of coffee, but almost choked. The coffee was so strong that if he didn't already have hair on his chest, it would have put some there. He tried to cover the bitter flavor with a bite of sausage, but it was so overcooked and dried out he could barely chew it.

The meal was a total and complete disaster. And one thing was absolutely clear. Lexi *did not* know how to cook.

If he had a choice, he would dump the whole thing down the sink, or do like he had when he was a kid and feed it to the dog. Unfortunately, they didn't have a dog, and she was gazing at him with such a hopeful look on her face, he didn't have the heart to hurt her feelings. He pasted on a smile and said, "Delicious."

He wasn't sure what brought on this sudden attempt at domesticity, but, mind-boggling as it was, he gave her credit for the effort. He forced down every last bite of eggs and sausage, stopping just short of licking his plate clean, and he even asked for a refill on his coffee.

"That was really good. Thanks." He stood to clear his place, but she stopped him.

"You sit. I'll do it."

She cleared away his dirty dishes and set them in the dishwasher. "I was thinking of making lamb for dinner," she said.

If it was even half as bad as breakfast, he didn't

think his stomach could take it. "Why don't you let me cook dinner?"

She frowned. "Why?"

He could see that he was walking a very delicate line here. One wrong step and he would hurt her feelings. "It's only fair that we split the household chores while we're here. Don't you think?"

"But I'm your wife. I'm supposed to take care of you."

That was the part he didn't get. Hadn't they agreed that this wasn't a real marriage? That this was a business deal? This was the last thing he expected. "Why, Lexi?"

The space between her brows furrowed. "Because that's what wives do."

Real wives maybe, not pretend ones. Maybe she had caught a bug and wasn't feeling well, or she was a little off due to jet lag. "You don't have to."

"But I *want* to."

What was he supposed to say to that? You can take care of me in the bedroom anytime you like, but otherwise leave me alone? That was just…sleazy.

It was obvious that a sexual relationship was a really bad idea. And he hoped like hell that this desire for domestic bliss would wear thin. They would get back to Houston and settle into a life of servants and chefs, and live amicable but very separate lives.

"If it means that much to you, you can make dinner," he said.

She sat back down at the table across from him, wearing a smile so full of relief it worried him.

What the hell was going on?

"So, what did you want to do today?" she asked. "We could walk to the village, or hire a car to take us on a tour of the island."

"Actually, I was thinking of just hanging out by the pool."

"Oh. Well, that sounds like fun."

He meant alone. As in, by himself. He hadn't even entertained the idea that she would want to spend the day with him. He figured they would just go their separate ways. But what was he supposed to say? Leave me the hell alone?

This was just too weird.

He rose from his chair and she stood up, too. "I'm going to take a shower."

"And I have to clean this mess. Meet you outside in thirty minutes?"

She looked so eager, so desperate to please him, all he could do was smile and say, "I can hardly wait." But he felt as if he'd climbed out of bed into an episode of *The Twilight Zone*.

Six

When Mitch was gone, Lexi collapsed back down into her chair, dropped her head in her hands and blew out a relieved breath. Talk about stressful. Making Mitch think this marriage was real was going to be a lot harder than she'd anticipated. Especially if he refused to cooperate. She had the feeling that in her attempt to impress him with her domestic skills, she might have overplayed her hand just the tiniest bit.

Thank goodness Tara had answered the phone when Lexi called—considering it had been after midnight, Houston time—and knew how to make scrambled eggs. Although it had still taken Lexi a dozen eggs and six tries to get it right. But part of that was due to the fact that she wasn't sure how to work the electric stove to get the proper heat settings.

It wasn't that she had never wanted to learn to cook, it was just that her father would never allow it. That was what they had servants for. He considered cooking and cleaning beneath her. She was sure it would be fun once she got the hang of it.

There was a leg of lamb thawing on the counter that Tara assured her would be a no-brainer, and tomorrow for breakfast, she might even try something complicated, like pancakes.

She walked to the stove, grabbed the pan of leftover eggs and was about to dump them down the sink when she realized her stomach was feeling marginally settled. She picked up a fork and took a bite, gagged and spit it directly into the sink.

They were awful. Yet Mitch had sat there straight-faced and eaten every bite. Even told her they were delicious. Though she wasn't supposed to have any, she poured herself a splash of coffee and gave it a taste. It was even worse than the eggs.

No wonder he'd suggested that he make dinner. He probably thought she was trying to poison him. She would have to be sure that she made dinner extra special. Maybe then he would think that breakfast had been a fluke and she wasn't completely useless.

She loaded the rest of the dishes and the frying pan into the dishwasher and filled the receptacle with the liquid dish soap she found under the sink, giving the dishes an extra squirt just to be safe. It took her a few minutes to figure out the digital display, but after randomly pressing buttons, she eventually got it running. It was amazing all of the things she didn't know how to do, but she was determined to figure them out. To be the perfect wife. The perfect partner.

However, one thing she definitely had to avoid was sleeping in Mitch's bed. She woke this morning with her stomach in knots, and barely made it to her own bathroom before she vomited. Mitch was bound to get suspicious if he realized she was tossing her cookies every morning. Every day she didn't tell him about the baby she risked making an even bigger mess out of things. But if things went according to plan, by the time she finally did tell him, he would be so happy, and love her so much, he wouldn't even care that she'd kept it from him.

Her baby's welfare depended on it.

Mitch showered, changed into his swim trunks, then headed to the kitchen to grab a soda on his way out to the pool. He stopped short in the doorway when he saw Lexi on her hands and knees, wearing a white beach cover-up, amid an ocean of thick white soap bubbles on the kitchen floor. She was trying frantically to wipe them up with a dish towel, but wasn't doing much more than pushing the suds around, and it was starting to overflow into the living room.

"What the hell happened?" he asked.

Startled, she looked up at him. "I don't know. Something is wrong with the dishwasher."

He looked over and saw that suds were continuing to ooze out from underneath the unit. He slipped and slid his way across the soapy floor and hit the cancel button. "Why didn't you shut it off?"

Only after the words were out, and he saw Lexi's wounded expression, did he realize how harsh he'd sounded. She looked at the dishwasher, then up at him and shrugged helplessly. It was then that he realized, she probably didn't know *how* to shut it off.

Keeping his voice calm, he asked, "How did this happen?"

"I told you, it's broken," she said. "I went to change and when I came back out, there was soap everywhere. You can bet the rental company is going to hear about this."

He had a pretty good idea what had happened, and it was in no way the rental company's—or even the dishwasher's—fault. "What kind of soap did you use?"

"The bottle under the sink," she said, in a tone that suggested he was dim for even asking.

He opened the cupboard and pulled out the soap sitting right in the front. "This one?"

"Yes, that one," she snapped. "Dish soap, for washing dishes."

"That's not for a dishwasher."

She frowned. "What do you mean? It says it is right on the label."

He reached back into the cupboard and extracted a box of granulated dishwasher detergent. "This is for the dishwasher. It doesn't suds up like regular dish soap."

"Oh," she said, pulling her lip between her teeth, looking mortified by her error. Once again, Mitch couldn't help but feel sorry for her. At least she was trying. How could he expect a woman who had probably never washed a dirty dish in her life to know how to run a dishwasher?

"Sorry," she said, her cheeks blushing bright pink.

He shrugged. "It's an honest mistake. No big deal."

She looked helplessly around at the mess she had created, as though she didn't have the first clue how to fix it. And though he felt like a complete degenerate for it, the only thing he could think about was getting her naked, laying her down and rolling around with her until they were both all slippery. Then he would…probably have his head examined.

"Why don't you go out by the pool," he told her. "I'll clean this up."

"It's my mess," she said.

Yes, and he had the feeling that if he left her alone to deal with it, she would only manage to make things worse. Besides, it would be advantageous to both of them if they weren't within mauling distance of each other.

"You're not here to wait on me hand and foot," he said. "You made breakfast, it's only fair that I clean up."

"Are you sure?" she asked, looking relieved for a valid excuse to bail on the situation.

"I'm sure. I'll have this cleaned up in no time."

"Okay." She rose to her feet, her legs all soapy, and tiptoed her way carefully across the floor, so she didn't slip and fall. "I'll see you outside."

No time ended up being over an hour, and he still hadn't been able to get all of the soap residue off the floor. He would just have to warn Lexi to be careful so she didn't slip while she was making dinner.

Though it wasn't noon yet, he felt he'd earned himself a cold beer. He grabbed one from the fridge, put his sunglasses on and headed out to the pool. Lexi lay in a lounge chair on the opposite side, sunning herself. Her eyes were shaded behind dark, designer sunglasses and she was wearing what looked like a very skimpy, pale bikini.

Wait a minute....

He slid his glasses down his nose to get a better look at her, and as his eyes adjusted to the bright sunshine, he realized she was in fact not wearing a pale bikini, skimpy or otherwise.

Lexi wasn't wearing anything at all.

Eyes closed behind her sunglasses, the late-morning sun drenching her skin at a very comfortable seventy-five degrees, Lexi tried to shake off the mortification of failing at the simple task of working the dishwasher. She should have called Tara before she went anywhere near it. She also should have stayed in the kitchen and helped Mitch clean, but she was too embarrassed. And no doubt if she had stayed, she would have done that wrong, too, and looked even more inept than she already did. How could she expect him to take her seriously, to consider her a good wife, if she couldn't even negotiate her way around a kitchen? She would have to make an absolutely perfect dinner.

More than an hour had passed when she finally heard Mitch open the patio door. She peeked through half-closed lids and saw that he was walking in her direction. A shadow robbed the sunshine as he hovered over her. "What the hell do you think you're doing?" he asked, his harsh tone making her jolt with surprise.

Was this some sort of trick question? "S-sunbathing?"

She could see by his exasperated expression that it wasn't the answer he wanted to hear.

"Yes, I can see that," he said. "What I would like to know is why you're naked."

"Technically, I'm not naked. I have bottoms on." More exasperation on his face, so she added, "I don't like tan lines. Besides, everyone in Europe sunbathes topless."

"You're a senator's daughter. I would think you'd know better."

She looked around. "Who's going to see me? We're in the middle of nowhere."

"That's not the point."

Then what was the point? What man didn't enjoy seeing his wife sunbathing topless?

The kind who married his wife for business. One who found her so physically unattractive, the only place he cared to see her naked was in a dark bedroom, where he could pretend she was someone else.

She felt sick all the way down to her soul. She pulled herself up from her chair, grabbed the towel she'd been lying on and wrapped it around herself. "I'm sorry that you find my body so offensive."

"Lexi, that isn't what I—"

"I'll be sure to keep it appropriately covered from now on," she assured him, nose in the air, giving him the cold and bitchy routine so he wouldn't hear the hurt in her voice. She turned to walk away, but Mitch wrapped a hand around her upper arm to stop her.

"I swear you're the most insecure woman I've ever met," he said. "And you're making it really hard for me to do the right thing."

The right thing? What was that supposed to mean? She tried to tug her arm free. "Let go."

Instead, he yanked the towel from around her and scooped her up. She let out a shriek as he flung her like a sack of potatoes over one shoulder and carried her toward the sliding glass door that led to his bedroom.

She wiggled, trying to get loose, but he only held on tighter. "What are you doing?"

"I could tell you that you're beautiful and desirable until I'm blue in the face, but you probably wouldn't believe me."

Okay, so maybe he didn't find her *completely* undesirable.

She pounded on his back with her fists, which was about as effective as hitting a boulder with a feather. "So, you pull a caveman routine instead?"

He slid the door open and carried her into his bedroom. Despite his brutish and uncivilized behavior, a shiver of excitement rippled through her. After all, it had been her plan to keep him in the bedroom as much as possible.

He slid her off his shoulder onto her back on the mattress and knelt beside her, a look of pure mischief in his eyes. "You won't listen to me," he said. "So, I'm just going to have to show you."

Mitch spent the rest of the morning and a good part of the afternoon showing Lexi just how beautiful and desirable he thought she was. And boy, was he good at it. Every time she tried to climb out of bed, he would pull her back in and start convincing her all over again. When she finally insisted she had to put the lamb in the oven or it wouldn't be ready in time for dinner, he reluctantly let her go. She wobbled into the kitchen on spaghetti legs, and every inch of her skin hummed with sexual satisfaction.

At this rate, it wouldn't be long before she could tell him about the baby.

Following Tara's instructions to the letter, Lexi seasoned the lamb shank and popped it in the oven. And though it took a minute of pushing buttons, the oven finally beeped and turned on. She peeled the potatoes and carrots next, then put them aside to add to the roasting pan forty minutes before the lamb was done. Until then, she didn't have much to do, so she went looking for Mitch.

She found him sacked out in a lounge chair by the pool, sleeping so deeply, he was snoring. It looked as though she'd worn the poor guy out. For a second, she considered all the creative ways she could wake him, most using her mouth, but he looked so peaceful, she didn't have the heart.

Instead, she stretched out in the chair beside him to get some sun, but her eyes felt heavy and in no time she drifted into a deep sleep, and had strange and erotic dreams about Mitch. Hazy, disjointed images of bare skin and feelings of intense sexual sensation flooded her. She could smell him, taste the flavor of his mouth and skin. She could feel the weight of his hands touching her, her hair tangled in his fingers, the flex of her muscles as she took him deep inside her body. The strum of sensation on her nerve endings.

Not a strum so much as a loud hum. And the hum grew louder, the sound filling her head until it was more annoying than arousing. A sharp, piercing bleat.

Her eyes flew open and she realized the sound wasn't in her dream. It was coming from the house, through the open door that led to the kitchen…and was that *smoke* she was seeing?

Wide awake now, she jumped from the chair, grabbed her cover-up and tugged it on as she dashed for the house. She was stunned by what she encountered in the kitchen.

Acrid smoke hung in the air, the oven sat open and empty and the pan the roast had been in was sitting in the sink under a flow of water. She could only assume that the black lump was the charred remains of the lamb shank. Mitch stood in the middle of the room in his swim trunks, fanning the smoke detector with a broom.

Oh, God, what had she done this time?

Mitch finally looked over and saw her standing there, watching him. He flashed her a smile and said, "The lamb is done."

After the dishwasher fiasco this morning, there didn't seem to be much point in trying to blame it on the oven. She had obviously screwed up again. Only this time, instead of flooding the house, it looked as though she'd nearly burned it down.

They had made some real progress today, and now

she'd ruined it. She couldn't even imagine what he must be thinking, and she wondered how long it would be before she and the baby were out on the street.

Mitch swung the broom around and, using the handle end, gave the smoke detector a solid whack. It gave one final bleat, then fell silent. Which was even worse than the deafening screech.

She opened her mouth to say something, apologize maybe, but words escaped her.

Mitch walked over to the sink and turned off the tap, looking down at the soggy remains of dinner. "We should probably open a few windows to let the smoke out."

"I'll get the family room," she said, eager to skulk away in shame. This could go one of two ways. He would be completely exasperated with her and make her feel like a total dope, or he would be understanding and sweet, all the while thinking that she was a lost cause.

She honestly wasn't sure which would be more humiliating.

When every window on the main floor was open, she walked back to the kitchen where Mitch was closing the oven and shutting it off. She couldn't tell if he was angry, or just resigned to the fact that he'd married a domestic disaster.

She gestured to the sink, taking a feeble stab at humor. "Was the lamb thirsty, or is this your way of telling me it's too dry for your taste?"

"I couldn't find the lid or fire extinguisher, so this was the only way to douse the flames."

Flames? It had actually been on fire?

Just when she thought she couldn't be more embarrassed, she discovered a whole new level of humiliation. "I don't suppose you would believe me if I said the lamb was supposed to catch on fire."

He cracked a smile.

"So, what did I do wrong this time?" she asked, even though she wasn't sure she wanted to know. She couldn't imagine he would ever let her near the kitchen again, much less cook something.

"The oven was on broil instead of bake."

Which meant what, exactly? She thought meat was supposed to broil. Her confusion must have been obvious because he added, "Bake warms the entire oven uniformly and allows food to cook slower. Broil is a direct flame right over the pan and cooks things much faster. Obviously."

Something she would have known if she'd ever used an oven before.

"I'm sorry I murdered dinner," she said.

He shrugged, again like it wasn't a big deal. "Unless you're a pyromaniac, which I seriously doubt, it was an honest mistake."

She wanted to believe he felt that way, but he had to be realizing how truly useless she was. What would her next honest mistake be? Accidental poisoning?

Maybe there was a reason her father had kept her so sheltered. Maybe he could see that left to her own devices, she was a danger to herself and others.

"I suppose it's obvious that I've never cooked before. Or used a dishwasher."

"Seriously?" he asked, trying to look surprised, but he was a terrible liar.

She shot him a look.

"Okay," he admitted. "I sort of had that feeling."

"I appreciate that you choked down breakfast despite how awful it was."

He shrugged. "It wasn't *that* bad."

"Yes, it was. We would probably both be safer if you cooked from now on."

"What makes you think I can cook?"

"You can't be any worse than me. I should stay as far away as possible from the kitchen."

"How are you going to learn if you don't try?"

"I did try, and I almost burned the house down! I'm useless."

He huffed out an exasperated breath. "What is it with you and this low self-esteem? You are not useless. And if you really would like to learn, when we get back to Texas we'll enroll you in a cooking class."

She shook her head. "No, my father would never allow it. He considers it beneath me."

"Your father isn't the one calling the shots. You're married to me now, and you have a say in your own life."

At first, she thought he was just making fun of her, but then she realized he was serious. Unfortunately, it wasn't that simple. "If he finds out, he'll be furious, and you still need his senatorial support."

"Let me worry about that."

He would risk his relationship with her father just so she could have a couple of cooking lessons? She narrowed her eyes, still not sure if she could trust him, wondering if this was some twisted game to him. "You're serious?"

"Yes. Very serious." He folded his arms across his chest and leaned against the counter. "Out of curiosity, what else has your father kept you from doing?"

She considered his question for a minute, then said, "It would probably be easier to tell you what he *did* let me do, since it's a far shorter list."

Mitch shook his head. "My father could be a real bastard, but I'm beginning to wonder if I didn't have it so rough, after all."

It was the first time he had ever said anything to her about his family. Of course, she had never really asked. "What did he do to you?"

"Suffice it to say, the slug to the jaw I took from Lance was nothing in comparison."

"Your father *hit* you?"

"On a regular basis. But it sounds worse than it was. I got over it."

Why did she get the feeling he really hadn't?

"So, what are we going to do about dinner?" he asked.

She looked over at the sink, at the remains of the lamb shank. "Don't look at me. I'm not going anywhere near the stove until I get those lessons."

"In that case, why don't we get dressed and go into the village?"

That sounded like the perfect solution to her. "Give me fifteen minutes."

Seven

What the hell was wrong with him?

Mitch walked with Lexi down the dirt road to Tzia, the local village, wondering what the hell he'd been thinking today when he carried her into his bedroom. So much for treating this marriage like a business deal. But when she'd accused him of finding her repulsive, and he realized she actually meant it, that she wasn't just manipulating him, the hurt look she wore had done something to his brain. What choice did he have but to show her how wrong she was?

And what was all that crap about cooking lessons? Where the hell had that come from? He didn't care if she could cook or not. But again she had looked so helpless and dejected. He couldn't help but feel sorry for her. Which was probably exactly what she wanted. But there was a small part of him that kept wondering, what if it wasn't an act?

She'd reached for his hand as they left the villa, and what was he supposed to do? Refuse to hold it? Tell her he didn't think it was appropriate? They *were* married. He could feel himself getting sucked into…something, although as genuine as her feelings seemed to be, he couldn't shake the suspicion that she had ulterior motives. They had agreed this was going to be business and nothing more, and he was determined to stick to that. As soon as they got back to Texas. He figured by then they would have gotten this nagging sexual attraction out of the way and would both be sick of each other.

At least he hoped so.

They reached the village just before sundown. As they passed under the arch leading inside, the beauty of the architecture stunned him. They strolled down cobbled streets lined with shops, crowded bars, and outdoor cafés. There was even a gallery whose front window boasted the works of famous Greek artists such as Tsarouhis, Fasianos, and Stathopoulos.

After some browsing, they chose a quiet café at the north end of the village and sat outside under a thick blanket of stars. He ordered an ouzo and though he tried to convince Lexi to try it, she opted for a bottled water, instead. In D.C., she had always had a glass or two of wine with dinner.

"Are you sure you don't want something to drink?" he asked after the server left the table.

"I'm sure."

"Wine or beer?"

She smiled, a warm breeze blowing the hair back from her face. "Why, are you planning to get me drunk?"

If he'd learned one thing in the past couple of days, it was that he didn't need the aid of alcohol to have his way with her. They ordered their food, both choosing authentic Greek favorites, but when it came, Lexi just picked at it.

"You don't like it?" he asked.

"No, it's good. I'm just not very hungry."

As far as Mitch could tell, she'd barely eaten anything since they left the U.S., and maybe it was his imagination, but she looked thinner than she'd been that night in D.C. He didn't remember her collarbones being so pronounced and her cheeks so hollow. He knew she was insecure, but would she drive herself to the point of anorexia? Or what if she was sick? Something more dangerous than airsickness and jet lag?

"Is something wrong?" he asked.

His question seemed to surprise her. "No, why?"

"You've hardly eaten a thing since we left Texas. Are you sick?"

There was the slightest pause before she smiled and assured him, "I'm fine, really." But he couldn't escape the feeling that she wasn't being completely honest with him. Although, what reason would she have to lie?

By the time they finished eating, most of the shops had locked their doors and the bars looked over-crowded and smoky, so they headed back to the villa with nothing but the full moon to light their way. The air had cooled and it was so silent, Mitch could hear the thump of his own heart.

Once again, she reached for his hand and rather than fight it, he twined his fingers through hers.

She surprised him by asking, "Did your father hit Lance, too?"

His father wasn't a subject he liked to discuss, but in all fairness, he had been the one to bring it up earlier. "Lance, me, our mother—until she'd had enough, packed her bags and left."

"Your mother left without you?"

"As Lance likes to say, she had her reasons."

"My father never hit me, but in a weird way I wish he would have."

"No, you don't."

"At least then I would know that he felt *something*. After my mom died he just…shut down. I did everything I could to make him happy, everything he ever asked, but I still felt invisible."

If what she said was true, maybe she didn't have the spoiled and pampered life after all. Maybe she was just as bitter and confused as everyone else. Or maybe she was one hell of a good actress. Either way, this conversation was getting a little too personal. She needed to understand that when they got back to Texas, things would change.

But what if she didn't understand that? What if, God forbid, she thought she was falling in love with him? He knew how it was for women like Lexi. They decided on something they wanted and went after it with a vengeance, all pistons firing. Right up until the second they got bored and found a new toy to amuse them.

"We should probably talk about how things will be when we get back to Texas," he said.

She gazed up at him, her skin luminous in the moonlight. "What things?"

"Us. Our relationship."

"Okay."

"I just think I should be clear about a few things. I'm a very busy man, and I like to do things, to live my life, a certain way. You should know that I don't intend to change."

She nodded silently, but he had the distinct impression he'd hurt her feelings. If he had, he was sorry for that, but it was important they were both clear on the way things would be.

"As we agreed before, this is a business deal. Nothing more."

"Of course," she said, but he could swear there

was a slight waver in her voice. An edge of disappointment. Maybe she really believed things had changed. Well, that wasn't his problem.

Then why did he feel so damned guilty?

She was silent the rest of the walk home. When they walked in the door, he expected that they would go their separate ways, to their own beds, but she stunned him by keeping hold of his hand and leading him to his bedroom. The sex was so passionate and intense, for a while he almost forgot that it wasn't real. As she lay naked beside him, her body curled around his, the idea of this ending seemed almost inconceivable. But he had never been one to mistake sex for affection or love. When she tired of the arrangement and pulled her inevitable disappearing act, he wouldn't be sorry to see her go.

Though Mitch's words stung and she seriously considered giving up, Lexi chose to disregard what he'd said about their marriage and forge ahead with her plan.

They spent the better part of the next six days in bed, or in various other places, having sex. And when they weren't climbing all over each other, or collapsing with sheer exhaustion, they sunned themselves by the pool or went for walks and explored the shops in the village. Sometimes they just talked about his work, or their families. There was so much about him she didn't know—and wanted to learn.

As the days passed, she slowly began to realize that not only did she have real feelings for Mitch, she was almost positive she was falling in love with him. But since she had never been in love before, she couldn't be one hundred percent sure. She only knew that it had to be something very special, and she didn't doubt that he was feeling it, too.

Since that night walking back from the village, he hadn't said a word about the marriage being just business. Instead, he'd shown his affection for her in a hundred little ways.

She was confident that in a week or so, if all continued to go well, she would be able to tell him about the baby. Then she could finally stop feeling as though she was walking on eggshells, constantly conscious of everything she said and did.

She could finally relax and be happy.

Their last night in Greece, she lay beside Mitch, listening to his deep, heavy breathing as he slept, knowing she should get up and go to her own room, but feeling too lazy to move. She always waited until he was asleep to slip away. As much as she would have loved to spend all night with him, she was still getting sick every morning. Soon though, he would know about the baby, and she could stop hiding. But for now, she really needed to get up.

Five more minutes, she told herself, letting her eyes drift shut and cuddling up against Mitch's side.

When she opened her eyes again, sunshine was

pouring in the windows. Mitch was behind her, his breathing slow and deep as he slept, but one part of his anatomy was already wide awake.

As she was considering the most pleasurable way to wake the rest of him, she felt a familiar lurch in her stomach. She broke out in a sudden cold sweat and a wave of nausea overwhelmed her. Swallowing back the bile rising in her throat, she slid out of bed as quietly as possible and pulled on her nightgown. There was no time to make it to her own bedroom. She had no choice but to use Mitch's bathroom. She reached the commode just as her stomach violently emptied. The spasms were so intense, she was convinced she would look down and find an internal organ or two floating around. When she was finished, her entire body felt limp and shaky. She sat on the floor and rested her face against the cool tile wall.

"Are you all right?"

Lexi's eyes flew open. Mitch was standing in the doorway, wearing only his boxers, his hair mussed from sleep, concern etched on his face. Damn it! She should have shut and locked the door.

"I'm fine." She reached over and flushed the commode, but it was obvious that she'd been sick.

"No, you're not." He grabbed a washcloth from the towel bar and soaked it with cool water from the tap. He wrung out the excess and handed it to her. She wiped her face with it, feeling the nausea beginning to pass. She would be completely fine in an hour or so.

He reached over to feel her forehead, but she held up a hand to stop him. "I don't have a fever. I'm okay."

"What's going on?" he asked.

"Must be something I ate," she lied, and she could see he wasn't buying it.

"I know something is wrong. You've hardly eaten anything all week, you've lost weight, and every morning you look pale and exhausted. I want the truth."

He knew. She could see it on his face that he'd already figured it out for himself. Or at least suspected. She had the feeling that her saying the words was a formality at this point.

Maybe this was a good thing. The longer she put it off, the harder it was going to be, right? The more it would sound like a lie. And he didn't look upset, exactly. More concerned than angry, so maybe it would be okay.

She took a deep breath, blew it out, and finally said the words she had been holding on the tip of her tongue for more than a week. "I'm pregnant."

"Pregnant?"

She could not have prepared herself for the look of dumbfounded shock on his face. Whatever he might have thought was wrong with her, pregnancy had clearly never crossed his mind. And if his reaction was any indication, everything would *not* be okay.

"You didn't think to mention this before?" he asked, his voice low and quiet, but she could see that he was ready to explode. And could she blame him?

He'd said it himself, he didn't want to bring a child into this. Had she really thought a week of fantastic sex was going to make him change his mind? Make him fall madly in love with her?

She felt as if she might be sick again.

"I only found out for sure a few days before we left," she said, knowing it was a pathetic excuse. "I was waiting for the right time to tell you."

"That's what this has all been about, hasn't it?"

"All what?"

"The cooking and the cleaning. The sex. Did you think you could manipulate me?"

Her heart sank. What was she going to tell him? No? Lie to him again? She had done that, just not in the way he thought. Not so sneaky and underhanded. "It wasn't like that, I swear. I wanted you to see that I could be a good wife."

He looked so disgusted with her, so…violated. "I didn't marry you so I could have a wife. I only did it for your father's support."

And that was her life in a nutshell. She was only as useful as her political connections. No words could have cut deeper or stung more.

"Does Lance know?" he asked.

Lance? Why would he think that she would go running to his brother? "No, of course not."

"And he never can," Mitch said.

His words took her aback. What the hell was that supposed to mean? How could he not find out, eventually? Did Mitch expect her to give the baby up, or even worse, terminate? Was he that cold and heartless, or so arrogant that he believed the choice was his alone?

What did his brother have to do with this, anyway? This was between her and Mitch. "Who cares if Lance does find out? What's he going to do about it?"

The veins at his temple pulsed. "You can't mess with people's emotions that way, Lexi. He and Kate are happy. Something like this could tear their marriage apart. I refuse to let that happen."

How could she and Mitch having a child ruin Lance's marriage? This didn't make any sense. "What are you asking me to do, Mitch?"

"We'll raise the baby as mine," he said.

Then it dawned on her. Their odd and confusing conversation suddenly made sense. He thought it was Lance's child. Lance, who she had barely kissed, much less slept with. It had never even occurred to Mitch that the baby was his.

Did he honestly believe that she would jump from Mitch's bed right into his brother's? Did he really have such a low opinion of her?

Obviously, he did. This past week, all the time they had shared, it meant nothing to him. He was using her for a good time, because he apparently believed that was all she was good for.

Her stomach lurched and she had to fight to keep from vomiting again. How had she gotten into this mess? Married to a man who considered her a garden-variety slut, one who jumped from one brother to the next as casually as she changed shoes. Even if she did try to tell him the truth, she doubted he would listen, or believe her. Or care.

She had been hoping they might have a real marriage. Not just hoping, but longing for it. She desperately wanted someone to really see her. To love her. But it was clear that Mitch would never be that man. He could never respect or love her, and all the pretending, all the seducing in the world would never change that. It would never alter the preconceived notion he had of her.

First rejected by her father, then by her husband. As long as she lived, she would never trust any man ever again.

Using the wall for support, she pulled herself to her feet. She swayed unsteadily for a second, then straightened her spine and faced Mitch. "If you'll excuse me," she said, brushing past him, but he grabbed her by her upper arm to stop her.

"From now on, I would appreciate it if you kept your hands to yourself."

She lifted her chin and met his eyes, so he wouldn't see how humiliated and cheap he'd just made her feel. "The truth is, you were hardly worth the effort. Looks like I married the wrong brother."

She could see that her arrow had hit its mark, but for some reason it only made her feel worse.

She yanked her arm free and stalked from the

room. She was stuck with a man who was arrogant, coldhearted and just plain mean.

On the bright side, she could spend the rest of her life making him as miserable as she was.

Mitch watched Lexi strut from the room, feeling more betrayed and disillusioned than he ever had in his life. He'd honestly believed that they had connected, that the dynamics of their relationship had shifted. He'd let himself consider that their marriage might be more than a business deal. But it had all been an act. She had used him.

How could he have been so foolish? How could he have let his guard down when all along he knew the kind of woman that she was? Because he had been thinking with something other than his brain, that's how.

Alexis Cavanaugh was a spoiled, heartless viper and that would *never* change.

At least now he knew why she had so readily agreed to marry him, and he was thankful that she had. Lance and Kate were happy and he refused to let Lexi's selfishness—her lack of concern for anyone but herself—ruin that. For all he knew, she might have conceived on purpose. Maybe she felt she needed a bargaining chip, a way to guarantee her marriage to Lance, but he had broken the engagement and married Kate. Mitch could only imagine what Lexi's next move would have been had he not offered to marry her, instead. Blackmail, maybe? Extortion?

He wondered what the senator would think if he knew what his daughter had been up to. Of course, for all he knew, she learned this sort of behavior from him. But Mitch couldn't let himself forget the old man's threat. *If you hurt my daughter, I'll ruin you.* He didn't have a choice but to make this work. For the company's sake.

She was his wife, God help him, and he was going to raise his brother's child the way he would his own, with the best of everything. He had never imagined being a father, especially at his age, but he didn't seem to have much choice. He had no reservations about running a multimillion-dollar company, but the responsibility of shaping a child's life terrified him. Probably because his own father had done such a bang-up job with him and Lance.

When Lexi grew bored and left them, which he had little doubt she would eventually do, he would reject everything he had learned from his own father and be the best single parent possible. He owed the kid that much. Someday, when the time was right, he would tell Lance and the child the truth, but until then, no one but he and Lexi would know.

That wasn't even the worst part. To keep up the ruse, so Lance didn't suspect the truth, Mitch and Lexi had no choice but to make their marriage look like a real one.

Eight

The trip home was the longest and most miserable in Lexi's life. It was raining as they boarded the ferry to the mainland and the ride was a choppy one, launching her already questionable stomach into turmoil. The first leg of their flight was delayed due to weather and they missed their connecting flight. They were stuck in the London airport for six hours waiting for the next available departure, and when they finally took off for Texas, the flight was so turbulent she spent most of it in the bathroom in a scene straight out of *The Exorcist*.

The entire time, Mitch didn't say a single word to her.

When they reached Houston, she was so relieved she felt like dropping to her knees and kissing the ground. She just wanted to go home and crawl into her own bed. But as they were climbing into the limo, Mitch reminded her that all of her things had been moved into his townhouse and that was her home now. On the bright side, he didn't seem any happier about it than she was. Her misery wasn't as hard to swallow when she knew he was right there with her.

Located on a golf course in what was by far the most affluent neighborhood in Maverick County, Mitch's townhouse was anything but small. The front door opened into a foyer and spacious living area. It smelled of furniture polish and faintly of Mitch's aftershave. The decor, to her surprise, was very homey and welcoming. Not what she would expect from a house occupied exclusively by a man.

There was a formal dining room and enormous kitchen with every modern device known to man. On the countertop sat a huge bouquet of flowers, two champagne glasses and a bottle of sparkling fruit juice chilling on ice. Beside it was a note penned in Tara's handwriting that read, *Congratulations and welcome home!*

At Mitch's questioning look, she said, "It's from Tara, my assistant."

He gestured to the nonalcoholic drink. "I guess it's safe to say she knows you're pregnant."

"She's my best friend. I tell her everything." Well, almost everything.

"That's sad," he said.

"What? That I tell her everything?"

"No, that you have to pay someone to be your best friend."

How did he always manage to hit the rawest nerve? But she refused to let him know that he'd hurt her feelings. She lifted her nose at him and said, "That's a little hypocritical coming from a man who had to buy his wife."

She braced herself for a sarcastic comeback, but instead, the hint of a smile tipped up the corner of his mouth, catching her off guard.

"Your room is on the second floor," he said. He backtracked through the house to where he left her bag by the stairs. He grabbed it and started up, and she followed him.

"Dry cleaning is picked up and dropped off Mondays and Thursdays. It will be your responsibility to see that it's left on the porch."

"Fine."

"I have a cleaning service in Monday, Wednesday and Friday."

"What about a cook?"

"I'm not home enough to warrant it. I usually eat out or order in. But if you want to hire someone, I won't object. And of course when we move, we'll need a full-time staff." He led her to the first room on the left. As far as she could see, there were three other bedrooms.

It was a typical spare bedroom, with gender-neutral furnishings and decor, but Tara had placed several of her things from her bedroom at her father's estate around the room. Photos and keepsakes mostly, as well as her books.

She peered into the walk-in closet and saw that Tara had also arranged all of her clothes and shoes, and in the bathroom she found her makeup and toiletries.

Mitch stood in the doorway watching her. "Is it satisfactory?"

It was more than adequate, but she said, "I suppose, if this is the best you can do."

He folded his arms across his chest. "Well, the master suite is larger, but then, you would have to share it with me."

Like *that* would ever happen. "Where is your room?"

"Why? Are you planning another midnight visit?"

"Actually, I need to know so I can avoid it."

He flashed another wry grin. "End of the hall on the right. The third floor is the den and my office. I would appreciate it if you didn't go up there."

Which meant that would be the first place she investigated.

"Just up the road is the community center. There's an exercise room and tennis courts. There's also a pool, although I'll warn you that bathing suits are not optional. Unless you want to get yourself arrested."

"Don't worry, I'll only walk around naked inside the house."

He didn't look as though he believed her, which would make actually doing it all the more fun.

"I'll need a space for Tara to work."

"She can have the room across the hall. I'll call my real estate agent so we can start house hunting."

She still didn't see the need for anything bigger than this, but he was the one paying the bills, so who was she to argue? "I'd like to unpack and change, and I have a few phone calls to make," she told him.

"Okay," he said, but he didn't move. At her questioning look he added, "Oh, did you want me to leave?"

"Please."

"I should probably check in with my girlfriend, anyway. Let her know I arrived home safely."

She wondered if he really did have a girlfriend, then figured he probably just said he did to annoy her. If he cheated on her and her father found out, Mitch could kiss his support goodbye. She smiled sweetly and said, "You mean the girlfriend who needs occasional reinflation?"

He smirked. "I'll be unpacking if you need me," he said as he left, closing the door behind him.

She sat on the bed and looked around. She would have to thank Tara for setting up her room. It made her feel a lot less like an interloper.

She turned on her cell phone and found she had half a dozen messages from her father and two from Tara. Since she wasn't quite ready to face her father yet, she called Tara first. They hadn't spoken since before the kitchen disaster—she'd been too embarrassed to admit how she had botched Tara's seemingly simple instructions.

She dialed and Tara answered on the first ring. "Welcome home! Did you see your surprise?"

"I did, thanks. And thank you for arranging all of my personal things."

"I'd love to take credit, but that was your husband's idea."

It was weird enough when she thought of Mitch as her husband, but to hear someone else say it felt like the final nail in her coffin. "That must have been before he decided he hates my guts."

"Oh, my gosh! What happened? I thought things were going really well."

"They were. He didn't even seem to care that I completely botched breakfast, flooded the kitchen, and nearly burned the house down making dinner. And the sex? Amazing. Everything was great, right up until the second I told him I'm pregnant."

"Oh, no, Lex. Was he really that upset?"

"I don't think it was the baby so much as the fact that he thinks it's Lance's."

"He what!?" she shrieked, obviously outraged. "You told him the truth, right?"

"There didn't seem to be much point. I doubt he would have believed me. He apparently thinks he knows the kind of person I am. I figure, why shatter his illusion?"

"Oh, Lex, I'm so sorry."

"I guess the worst part was that I thought for the first time in my life, someone really saw me, you know? I thought he cared." Lexi was mortified to realize that she was welling up. Enough of this. She had to pull herself together.

"Maybe if you told him the truth—"

"There's no point now. I can never trust him again."

"You're going to have to tell him eventually."

Yes, but for now, she would make him suffer a bit. Make him as miserable as she was. "Could we talk about something else?"

"Sure, Lex," she said, sounding hurt. Why did it feel as though whatever Lexi said or did, it was never right?

They talked briefly about setting up a temporary office for Tara in the townhouse, and then she called her father.

In lieu of hello, he snapped, "Why didn't you call? You should have been home hours ago."

It was on the tip of her tongue to say, "Hi, Dad, nice to talk to you, too." But she had never had the courage to speak to him that way. One wrong move and he might shut her out completely. Stop calling altogether.

"Our flight was delayed due to bad weather," she said. "We just got home."

"Well, I was concerned."

Just not concerned enough about her to come to her wedding, or call her while she was in Greece.

"Would a call have been too much trouble?" he asked sharply.

She could have asked him the same thing, but of course she didn't. "No, Daddy. I'm sorry."

That took the edge off his tone. "How was your vacation?"

"Greece was wonderful." It was the company she could do without. Although she couldn't deny that they'd had several very good days.

"You, Mitch and I will be meeting for dinner tomorrow evening at the Cattleman's Club," he said. *Demanded,* really.

"I'll have to ask Mitch if he's available."

"If he wants my support, he will be. Seven o'clock. Don't be late. I'm flying in from D.C."

He was flying all that way just to have dinner? She wondered what she and Mitch had done to deserve that. "We'll be there."

They disconnected and she set her phone down. She should probably give Mitch the good news.

She changed into a T-shirt and cotton capri pants, then went looking for Mitch. She started to walk toward his bedroom, then changed her mind and decided this would be the perfect time to snoop upstairs. She tiptoed quietly so he wouldn't hear her, and what she saw as she reached the top took her breath away. The entire floor was one large, open room. At one end was Mitch's office, which consisted of a slightly cluttered desk, file cabinet and bookshelves lining one wall. Across the room was a media center with a huge flat-screen television and a whole cabinet full of electronic equipment. Not to mention a wet bar. Everything was dark polished wood with comfortable-looking chocolate-brown leather furniture. One hundred percent male.

She crossed to his office area, running her fingers across the back of his chair, wondering if she should take a peek inside his desk. Just to annoy him, of course.

"I should have known I would find you up here."

She turned to find Mitch standing at the top of the stairs, arms folded over his chest.

"I thought we agreed you wouldn't come up here."

She shrugged. "I believe you issued an order. I never agreed to it. This is nice, though. Very macho."

"Is there a particular reason you're up here?"

To annoy you. "I was looking for you."

"Really? Because I told you I would be in my room, unpacking."

"I must have forgotten."

"What did you want?"

"To warn you that my father has invited us to dinner at the Cattleman's Club tomorrow night at seven."

"I'll have to check my schedule."

"That's what I told him. He said that if you want his support, you'll be there."

"Well, then, I guess I'll be there."

"That's what I told him."

"My brother left me a message. He said that Kate would like you to join her for a welcome-to-the-family lunch on Thursday."

"Family?"

"She is your sister-in-law."

Oddly enough, Lexi hadn't even thought about that.

She had a family now—someone other than her father, that is. But she couldn't help wondering if it would be weird going out to lunch with the woman who had stolen her fiancé. "I'm not sure if that's a good idea."

His expression darkened. "You think you're better than her?"

"Of course not! Kate seems wonderful. I just thought it might be awkward."

"Fine, I'll tell Lance you don't want to go."

"I didn't say that. I'll go, okay?"

He shrugged, as though it didn't matter either way to him, yet she had the distinct feeling it did. "She said to meet her at the Cattleman's Club café at one."

She nodded, wondering how she was going to get there. If she asked Mitch to send a car for her, he would probably just accuse her of being spoiled. Unfortunately, her father had never allowed her to learn how to drive. Having his driver take her everywhere was just another way for him to keep track of her every move. Maybe Tara could drive her. And maybe, if she asked Tara nicely enough, she might teach Lexi to drive. She was twenty-four years old. It was high time she began asserting her independence.

"I talked to the real estate agent. We have a 10:00 a.m. appointment tomorrow. He said he has several properties to show us."

"That was quick."

"I called him last week and told him we'd be looking. The state of the economy being what it is, he said if we decide to buy, there's a huge selection right now. Building new would take considerably longer."

She shrugged. "Whatever you want. As long as I'm free by four."

"Why?"

"I have an appointment with my gynecologist."

His expression darkened. "Speaking of that, I think it would be best if we kept the...*situation* to ourselves."

She was tempted to tell him that the *situation* had fingers and toes and a beating heart, but she didn't see the point. He obviously wasn't ready to acknowledge the life growing inside of her. "Fine."

"Also, I think it would be best if people are led to believe that we're happy."

She pursed her lips. "Then maybe we should forget those cooking lessons and get me some acting lessons, instead."

"You don't give yourself enough credit. In Greece you had me snowed."

That's because I wasn't acting, you moron, she wanted to shout. But what good would it do? His mind was made up about her and she would never forgive him for it, so they were more or less at an impasse.

"Define happy," she said.

"I think we should act like newlyweds, show each other affection."

She narrowed her eyes at him. "How much affection?"

"I'm not suggesting we publicly maul each other. I'm talking about little things like holding hands, and maybe occasionally smiling at each other."

"But no kissing," she clarified. Not that she didn't enjoy kissing him. Quite the opposite. Every time his lips touched hers she got so hot her brain short-circuited. If that happened she might do something stupid, like sleep with him again. And because he did amazing things to her body, she knew once wouldn't be enough. If she slept with him too many times, she might begin to forget how awful he was.

"No kissing," he agreed.

Good.

So why did she feel disappointed that he hadn't put up at least a tiny fuss?

His cell phone rang and he looked at the display. "It's Lance. I have to take this."

"I'll be in the kitchen getting something to eat."

She brushed past Mitch and headed downstairs, hearing him call after her, "The fire extinguisher is in the pantry."

Smart-ass. She should burn the place down just to spite him.

"Welcome home," Lance said when he answered. "Did you get my message?"

"Yeah. In fact, I just talked to Lexi. She'll meet Kate for lunch." He didn't mention that Lexi hadn't looked all that thrilled with the idea. Mitch knew that she and her father looked down on people of Kate's past station in society.

"I'm glad," Lance said. "Kate is pretty excited about having a sister-in-law."

"Seriously?"

"The truth is, she credits Lexi for us finally getting together. If I hadn't planned to marry Lexi, Kate probably never would have quit, and I would still be walking around with my head in the clouds, not realizing how important she is to me."

That was an interesting way to look at it.

"Speaking of marriage," Lance said, "how was the honeymoon?"

"It was okay," Mitch told him, which wasn't a total lie. It had gone pretty well, right up until the moment Lexi showed her true colors. Unfortunately, if Mitch was honest about how truly miserable he was, not only would Lance feel guilty as hell, he might want to know why. It would be best for every-one involved if even Lance believed Lexi and Mitch were happy.

"Just okay?" Lance hedged.

"Better than okay," Mitch said. "I think this just might work out."

"I'm glad to hear it," he said, sounding relieved.

Mitch wasn't yet sure how he planned to handle the news of Lexi's pregnancy. Lance wasn't stupid. He would do the math and realize when she'd con-ceived. Mitch would just have to admit to his brother that he and Lexi slept together in D.C. He could lie and say they were drunk, claim they had been so out of it they had forgotten to use protection. He just hoped Lance wasn't too pissed at him, although Mitch wouldn't blame him if he was.

But that could wait a while, at least another month or two, until Lexi started to show.

"Any news about the fire?" he asked his brother.

"Whoever set it knew what they were doing. Darius hasn't been able to trace a thing."

"What does he think about Montoya? Is he even capable of pulling something like that off?"

"If he is, we'll find out."

Mitch couldn't help wondering if Lance was so determined to pin the fire on Alex Montoya that he would wrongly accuse an innocent man. "What if it wasn't him?"

"He's the only one with motive."

"We don't know that for sure, " Mitch countered.

"Hey, by the way," Lance said, "Darius asked that we meet him at his office next Wednesday evening."

"Did he say what for?"

"He said we had some business to discuss, but he wouldn't say more than that."

"Does it have something to do with the fire?"

"I don't think so."

"Sure, I'll be there." He was sure that by then he would need a night away from his wife—if they hadn't already killed each other.

Nine

The following morning Mitch and Lexi drove to the real estate agent's office to begin looking at houses. And though she still felt like death warmed over from a bout of kneeling to the porcelain gods, she put her best face on. The agent, Mark Sullenberg, was a friend of the family, which meant she and Mitch had to act happily married.

Unfortunately, he was really good at it.

There was barely a minute when he wasn't touching her, either holding her hand or casually draping his arm across her shoulders. He was so good, so charming and sweet to her, she started to forget they were only playing a role. It made her think of that week in D.C. and how perfect it had been, how naturally they had connected, which in turn made her feel depressed and lonely, because she knew she would never feel that way again.

She just prayed they would find a house soon, so they could go back to hating each other. But after looking at half a dozen homes, they hadn't found a thing either of them even remotely liked. They were all ultramodern in exclusive gated communities with lots of BMWs and luxury SUVs in the driveways. And they all looked the same. Lifeless and boring. By the sixth house, she could see that Mitch was getting frustrated and she was beginning to think that building new might be their only option.

"Can you show us something different?" Mitch asked Mark. "Something a bit more…"

"Traditional," she finished for him.

"Exactly," he said, looking surprised that she'd nailed it right on the head. "Something with some character."

"There is one property that recently came on the market," Mark said. "It's just outside of Maverick County. A renovated plantation house. The only problem is that it's located on ten acres of land, and you said you wanted to look in more of a suburban setting."

"How big is it?" Mitch asked.

"Fifty-five-hundred square feet. It used to be a horse farm, so there's a barn and stables."

That caught Lexi's attention. Her uncle on her

mother's side had kept horses when Lexi was a child. Though she had always wanted to learn to ride, her father would never allow it. Too dangerous, he'd decided. But her uncle would let her brush the horses and help feed and water them. The idea of owning a horse or two thrilled her.

She glanced over at Mitch, thinking she would reduce herself to begging if that was what it took to make him agree to at least look at it, but he appeared as intrigued as she was.

He shrugged and said, "Couldn't hurt to look at it."

They piled back into Mark's car for the twenty-minute ride, Lexi feeling uncharacteristically excited. For some reason, she had a really good feeling about this one.

"I'll warn you that it's a little run-down and overgrown," Mark told them. "When the owner died, there was a dispute with the will so it's been sitting empty for a while. It has a lot of potential, though."

They pulled off the road into a long, tree-lined driveway. He hadn't been kidding when he said it was overgrown. It would take a lot of work to get the yard in order. But Lexi couldn't keep her eyes off the house itself. It was…amazing. A huge, white Greek revival with pillars and balconies and black shuttered windows. She could just imagine herself in the evenings sitting on the long front porch drinking lemonade and watching the sun set, or playing with the baby in the shade of the trees.

She knew without a doubt, this was the one. This was home.

Mark pulled to a stop and they all climbed out. As he'd done before, Mitch took her hand, lacing his fingers through hers. But this time it was different. This time he really held on, as though he was brimming with pent-up excitement.

"It was built in 1895," Mark told them, "and completely remodeled about thirty years ago. It's a little rough around the edges, but an excellent investment."

She and Mitch stood there for a moment, side by side, hands clasped, gazing up at the remarkable structure. Lexi didn't know about Mitch, but she felt as though this was meant to be. As if, for the first time in her life, she'd finally come home.

"So, what do you think?" Mark asked.

"We'll take it," they said in unison, then looked at each other, startled that they were in complete agreement.

Mark laughed. "Wow, how's that for a consensus? You haven't even seen the inside."

"Well, then," Mitch said, giving her hand a squeeze, "let's see it."

Lexi knew at this point that it was only a formality, but they followed Mark up the porch and through the front door. The interior was a bit shabby and outdated, the kitchen and bathrooms in particular desperately needed updating, but all Lexi could see was the potential. Mitch must have felt the same way. When they concluded the tour he told Mark, "Let's write up an offer," and when they got back to the office to fill out the paperwork, instead of bidding low, he offered several thousand above the asking price.

Though she didn't let it show, she felt almost giddy with anticipation. They were buying a house. A house whose renovations she would help plan, and whose rooms she would decorate however she chose. She could hardly wait to get started.

She had never felt so…*alive*. As though an entirely new and amazing world was opening up to her.

"I'll submit this right away and hopefully we'll hear something in the next day or two," Mark told them as they were leaving. "I'll be in touch."

Though she was practically bursting with excitement when they were in the car on the way back to the townhouse, Lexi tried to hide it. An automatic defense mechanism she'd learned from dealing with her father. If he knew something was important to her, he would use it against her as leverage. A true politician.

Then Mitch asked, "So, you liked it?"

She could no longer contain herself. She blurted out, "I knew I wanted it the second we pulled into the driveway. If I had every house in the world to choose from, that's the one I would have picked."

"It's going to need a lot of work. It'll probably be months before we can move in."

"I would be happy living in it just the way it is."

He shot her a sideways glance. "The interior is a disaster. We're going to have to gut it and start from scratch. The renovations will go much faster if it's unoccupied."

Although she would be happy moving in there today, he made a good point. Especially with the baby coming. The sooner it was finished, the better.

"I'll start calling contractors today," he said.

"Shouldn't we wait until we know for sure that we got it?"

"Don't worry," he said, his tone a little smug. "We'll get it."

There were definitely advantages to being married to a man who was used to getting what he wanted.

"I'd like to get a horse or two," she said, prepared for an instant argument.

But Mitch said, "We could do that." Then he added offhandedly, "It would be a good atmosphere for raising kids."

It was the first time since she'd told him she was pregnant that he'd acknowledged the baby. She wondered how he would react when she told him the truth. Would it change his feelings for her? Make him dislike her a little less?

Probably not. Knowing Mitch, he would be even angrier, and hold it against her for the rest of her life. It would probably be in her best interest to at least wait until they had signed a mortgage to tell him the baby was really his. Just in case.

"Did you want to go to my appointment with me today?" she asked, unsure of what his reaction would be, and wondering how she would feel if he refused.

He was quiet for a moment, eyes on the road, then asked, "Do you want me to?"

She realized that yes, she did. Even though he didn't know it yet, this was his baby and he shouldn't miss out on anything. From the first pre-natal visit to the birth, she wanted him to be there for every minute of it.

He hates you. He thinks you're selfish and spoiled.

But if she denied him this opportunity, wouldn't she be proving him right?

Before she could talk herself out of it, she told him, "I want you to."

"Then I'll come," he said.

He reached over and turned the radio on to a country-western station, ending the conversation, yet she couldn't help but feel as though they had made some sort of progress today. Although progress toward what, she wasn't exactly sure.

The doctor's appointment wasn't at all what Mitch had expected. In fact, he hadn't known quite *what* to expect.

He figured they would take her temperature and blood pressure, which they did, and she was asked to pee in a cup. Typical doctor-visit stuff. What he hadn't been expecting was the internal exam.

Though he'd seen Lexi intimately on more than one occasion, and his first instinct was to do or say anything to annoy her, this just didn't seem the place, so he turned his back while she stripped from the waist down and got up on the table.

Even though the process went quickly, he gained a whole new respect for what women had to endure during a routine exam. Between all the poking and prodding and the giant cotton swab the doctor used for God only knows what, he felt grateful to have outdoor plumbing.

Then the doctor pulled out a piece of equipment that looked a lot like some recreational sex apparatus. It was long and narrow with a cord coming out one end that was attached to a monitor.

"This is an internal ultrasound," the doctor explained. "So we can get a better idea of the baby's development."

Lexi looked a little nervous so Mitch took her hand.

As the doctor inserted it, she gasped and said, "Cold," then winced a little as he made adjustments. Suddenly, up on the monitor popped a hazy black-and-white image.

"There's the fetus," the doctor said, pointing to a white area on the screen. "And these are the arms and legs."

Mitch didn't see anything but a fuzzy blob at first, but as the doctor gestured to the different body parts, it began to take shape. With its oversize head and stubby appendages, it looked more alien than human.

"This flutter is the heartbeat," the doctor told them.

"Can we hear it?" Lexi asked.

He turned the volume up and the rapid whoosh of the baby's pulse filled the room.

Mitch had never even considered being a father, and here he was listening to his baby's heartbeat, looking at its tiny form on a monitor.

Lance's baby, he reminded himself.

In a way, he felt as though he was stealing something invaluable from his brother, an opportunity to see his child develop. But he was sure that Lance and Kate would eventually have children and he would experience it all with her. This might be Mitch's only chance.

"Everything looks great," the doctor told her. "I'll see you in a month."

When they were back in the car and on their way home, Lexi sat so quietly gazing out the window that Mitch began to think maybe something was wrong. He couldn't help but ask, "Are you okay?"

"Seeing the baby, hearing the heartbeat. It suddenly seems so...*real*."

She looked so dazed and bewildered he wondered if the weight of the responsibility was finally sinking in. Wouldn't it be ironic if, now that he'd finally begun to accept the situation, she changed her mind and decided not to have it?

"You say that like it's a bad thing."

She looked over at him, surprise on her face. "No, of course not! I just…" She shrugged, then shook her head. "Never mind."

"Tell me," he said.

"You'll just make fun of me."

"I promise I won't make fun of you."

She studied him for a moment, as though she wasn't quite sure she could trust him. Finally she said, "I guess I'm just a little…scared."

He didn't think Lexi was scared of anything, and was surprised that she would admit it to him, of all people. "Scared of what?"

"Being a bad parent. What if I do everything wrong?"

It was on the tip of his tongue to say, "You probably will." But he didn't have the heart to knock her down when she looked so vulnerable and unsure of herself. She was opening up to him and he couldn't use that against her. Besides, there was always the very slim, one in a million chance that she would be a good mother and stick around. Maybe he should give her the benefit of the doubt.

So she would only disappoint him later? What was the point?

"You'll do the best you can," he told her, wishing he actually believed it, but Lexi seemed to buy it because she smiled.

A minute later, he pulled into his driveway and cut

the engine, but when he looked back over at Lexi she was frowning.

"What's wrong now?" he asked.

She turned to face him, looking almost nervous. "Mitch, there's something I need to tell you. Something you should know."

He had no idea what she was going to say, but he had the feeling he wasn't going to like it. "What?"

She hesitated, lip wedged between her teeth. Then she said, "About the baby…"

"What about it?"

"I thought you should know…"

She looked so nervous, he started to worry something was really wrong. "What are you trying to say?"

After another pause she finally said, "I just wanted to say thank you for coming with me today. For being a part of this."

And here he'd thought it had been something important. Half a dozen snarky comebacks were just dying to jump out, but instead he said simply, "You're welcome. Now, we better get inside and get ready or we'll be late for dinner. I get the distinct feeling your father isn't one to tolerate tardiness."

She smiled and nodded. "That's a fairly accurate assumption. I love my father, but to be honest, the sooner this evening is over and he flies back to D.C., the better, as far as I'm concerned."

Well, that was one thing they could agree on. So, why did he get the feeling there was something else? Something she wasn't telling him?

Ten

When Lexi and Mitch arrived at the Cattleman's Club to meet her father, her goal was to get in, eat dinner, and leave as fast as humanly possible. Which was odd because in the past she had cherished every moment her father would spare her. It seemed that lately she was no longer so desperate for his time or his approval. But Mitch needed his support, so she would be on her best behavior.

"Are you ready for this?" Mitch asked, holding out his hand for her to take.

She laced her fingers through his. Another few hours of pretending they were madly in love? She could hardly wait. At least now when he touched her it didn't feel so…unnatural. In a way it was kind of nice, even though she knew deep down that he hated her, or at the very least disliked her a lot.

"This way," the hostess said, gesturing toward the dining room door. They followed her, and as they entered the room, it took a few seconds for Lexi to process what she was seeing. Tables full of familiar people all smiling at them, balloons and streamers everywhere and a banner draped across the back wall that announced in huge block letters, *Congratulations Mitch and Lexi.*

Everyone shouted, "Surprise!" and the room erupted in laughter and applause.

She heard Mitch mumble, "Oh, shit," and thought, I couldn't have said it better myself.

Lance and Kate stood close to the door, beaming. He stepped forward and shook Mitch's hand.

"What did you do?" Mitch asked him.

"Don't look at me, bro. This was all Kate's idea. I couldn't talk her out of it."

"You had to have a wedding reception," Kate said, flush with excitement. She hugged Mitch, then pulled Lexi into a warm and affectionate embrace, and Lexi was so stunned she almost forgot to hug her back.

"But it wasn't just me," Kate said, nodding toward the door. "Your assistant was a huge help."

Lexi turned, and realized Tara was standing just off to one side of the door. She hadn't even seen her when they walked in.

She flashed Lexi a feeble smile and said, "Surprise."

She was the only one in the room who knew what a disaster the marriage was. No wonder she looked so apologetic.

"So, were you both surprised?" Kate asked.

Lexi nodded and Mitch said, "To quote the great Chevy Chase, if I woke up tomorrow with my head sewn to the carpet, I wouldn't be more surprised than I am now."

The room burst into laughter.

Someone handed Lexi and Mitch each a flute of champagne from a passing tray, and she realized everyone in the room already had their own glass.

Lance held his up in a toast. "To my little brother and his wife. May you live a long and happy life together!"

"Hear, hear!" everyone chanted, clinking their glasses together, and Lexi had no choice but to pretend to take a sip. As she studied the sea of faces before her, she couldn't help noticing that the one she had been expecting to see wasn't there. Her father.

Tara must have read her mind because she leaned close to Lexi and said, "The senator's secretary called a while ago to say he'll be a little late."

Didn't that just figure? He skips her wedding altogether and shows up late for the reception? She wondered why he bothered to show up at all. But she didn't have much time to think about it as a constant flow of friends, relatives and club members stepped forward to hug them or shake their hands and give their best wishes. Darius Franklin and his fiancée Summer Martindale, Kevin Novak and his wife Cara, Mitch's best man Justin Dupree. Even Sebastian Huntington and his daughter Rebecca were there. And those were just the people she recognized. She had no clue Mitch had so many friends.

A too-real wedding reception for a fake marriage. Did it get much worse? Lexi couldn't help thinking that this just might be the longest night of her life. But as the champagne flowed and the music played, she discovered herself getting caught up in the festivities. Mitch never once left her side, and if he wasn't holding her hand or draping an arm around her, he was touching her in some way.

Dinner was served around eight and halfway through the meal, Kate started to clink her glass with a fork, and then everyone joined in. Lexi had been to enough wedding receptions to know that it meant she and Mitch were supposed to kiss.

Mitch looked at her apologetically because he knew as well as she did that they had to make this look real. She held her breath as he cradled her face in his hand, leaned forward and laid a kiss on her that curled her toes and turned her brain to mush. The guests applauded, and she heard a couple of wolf whistles. After that, it seemed as though every five minutes the clinking started, and Mitch would be forced to kiss her yet again. Not that he seemed to mind, and she couldn't deny the man did fantastic things with his mouth.

He'd had several glasses of champagne with dinner, then after dessert, switched to whiskey. The more he drank, the more relaxed he became, and the more relaxed he became, the more affectionate he seemed to be. By the time they had their first dance together, he nearly had her convinced they were madly in love. The song playing was a slow one and he pulled her so close, gazed so tenderly into her eyes, she thought any minute he might drag her to the nearest broom closet.

"When we walked in here I thought this night was going to be a disaster," he said. "But I have to admit, it hasn't been so bad."

She'd thought the same thing, but she was actually having a great time.

"You might have to drive us home tonight," he warned her. "I think I may have had a few too many."

That could be a problem. "I can't."

He frowned. "You haven't been drinking, have you?"

"Of course not! What I mean is, I really can't. I never learned how to drive."

His eyes widened. "You're kidding."

She shook her head.

"Let me guess. Your father wouldn't allow it."

"It would have made it more difficult to keep me

under his thumb. I had a driver who took me wherever I needed to go."

Mitch shook his head in disgust. "No offense, but the more I learn about the senator, the less I like him."

His irritation stunned her, but she realized it was a nice change to have someone to defend her. "I can ask Tara to drive us."

"I'll call a car," he said. "And the first chance we get, I'm teaching you to drive."

"Seriously?" First cooking lessons, now driving? He was being almost too nice and understanding. Probably tomorrow, when he was sober, he would come to his senses and change his mind.

"Speak of the devil," Mitch said, gesturing toward the door with his chin.

She turned and saw that her father had arrived. He was watching Lexi and Mitch dance, and he didn't look happy.

"Is it my imagination," Mitch asked, "or does he look really pissed off?"

"It's not your imagination." She couldn't help wondering what she'd done this time, because when he looked like that, it was usually her fault. "I should go talk to him."

"You want me to come with you?"

"Maybe you'd better give us a few minutes alone." The last thing she needed was for her father to berate her in front of her husband. Not that she thought it was possible for Mitch to have a lower opinion of her than he already did, but why take a chance?

She crossed the room to where her father waited, forcing a smile, and said, "Hello, Daddy."

She hadn't expected a warm greeting, but she also hadn't expected him to clamp a hand around her upper arm and pull her to an unoccupied corner. He had never been one to get physical.

"What's the matter with you?" he said under his breath, but she had no idea what she'd done.

"I—I don't know."

Before the senator could respond, Mitch appeared at her side. He held a hand out for him to shake and her father had no choice but to let go of her arm.

"Senator Cavanaugh, I'm so glad you could finally make it." He was all smiles but his words had bite. He put an arm protectively around her shoulders and asked, "Is there a problem?"

"Yes, there's a problem. Lexi looks awful. Her skin is pale and she's obviously lost weight."

"You think so?" Mitch asked, looking down at her.

"I know my daughter, Mr. Brody, and I know something isn't right."

Sudden fear gripped her. With that invaluable senatorial support in mind, what if Mitch decided to break down and tell her father the truth? Instead, he looked at Lexi with one of those sizzling smiles and said, "She looks damned good to me." Then right in front of her father, he lowered his head and brushed his lips against hers, so soft and gentle and sweet that her knees went weak.

He eased back, and with his eyes locked on hers said, "Excuse us, Senator, but I'd like to dance with my wife."

Her father's stunned expression as Mitch took her hand and led her away gave Lexi far more satisfaction than it should have. When they were back on the dance floor, he said, "What the hell kind of man tells his daughter she looks awful at her wedding reception?"

"I probably looked happy."

"Isn't that the point?"

"I think it makes him feel threatened because when I'm happy about anything, he always says or does something to sabotage it."

"He's your father. He's supposed to *want* you to be happy."

Lexi shook her head. "The entire time I was growing up he talked about how he wished he'd had a son, but my mom died before they had the chance. He never said he resented me for being born a girl, but it was obvious he felt that way. As I got older, he started to talk about me getting married and giving him lots of grandsons. Like he only saw me as a baby-breeding machine or something."

"I guess that explains why he was so anxious to marry you off."

"Exactly." But he didn't want a grandson so badly

that he would tolerate her being an unwed mother. If she had a boy, she honestly wouldn't put it past him to try to take the baby and raise it himself.

"Is he still looking at us?" Mitch asked.

She looked past his shoulder and saw that her father was holding a drink and talking to Sebastian Huntington, but his eyes were on Lexi and Mitch.

"Yes, he's still looking."

A devilish smile curled the corners of Mitch's mouth and she was sure that any second he might sprout horns. "Then let's give him a good reason to feel threatened."

Before she could ask what he planned to do, he lowered his head and locked his lips with hers, kissing her so passionately, so deeply, she could swear she felt him hit her tonsils. She might have been embarrassed but her brain had ceased to function the instant his lips touched hers. When he finally pulled away, she was breathing hard and gripping his suit jacket with both hands.

"How did he like that?" Mitch asked, looking a little breathless himself.

She looked over just in time to see her father walk out the door. "Apparently he didn't, because he just left."

"Good riddance."

She looked up at him and smiled. "Thank you for rescuing me."

"You owe me big time," he said. "And I would be willing to accept sexual favors as payment."

She opened her mouth to speak, but before she had the chance he said, "Relax, I'm just kidding."

Oddly enough, she'd been about to ask, *What would you like me to do?* Instead she said, "Not that it wasn't fun to see my father knocked down a peg or two, but if you want his support you should really be careful what you say to him. He likes to play hardball, and he enjoys a good fight, but not at the expense of his pride."

"If getting his support means kissing his ass, I'm not sure I want it anymore."

Her breath caught in her throat. If Mitch didn't want her father's support, then why would he stay married to her? And if he left her, what would she do then? Crawl back to her father and beg him to take her in? What choice would she have?

"Of course, if I blow this, Lance will probably kill me," Mitch continued. "So, I don't really have much choice."

The surge of relief she felt was so complete she nearly collapsed. She couldn't help but feel she'd just dodged a bullet.

Mitch wasn't usually much of a drinker, but he had figured the more intoxicated he was, the less inclined he would be to attack Lexi the instant they stepped in the front door. And what a brilliant plan *that* had been. While he had managed to keep his hands to himself, he'd been lying in bed awake for the past hour staring at the ceiling with a boner that just wouldn't quit. But what did he expect when he spent half the night with his hands all over her and the other half with his tongue down her throat?

On the bright side, they seemed to have everyone at that party convinced that they were happy as clams and having the time of their lives.

He rolled over and the sensation of the sheets sliding against his hard-on was almost enough to set him off. He could always take care of matters himself, but how sad was that? Very, considering he had a gorgeous wife just down the hall and he couldn't make love to her.

Couldn't or wouldn't? He was the one making the rules. He had told her that their marriage wouldn't be more than business, and he was beginning to think that as far as dumb moves went, that just about topped them all.

He couldn't help but wonder if Lexi was lying in her bed, staring at the ceiling, feeling as sexually frustrated as he was.

He heard a noise coming from the first floor, the screech of the kettle whistling. He sat up in bed. Though normally boiling water wouldn't cause him alarm, he knew Lexi could find a way to turn even making tea into a disaster of biblical proportions.

He jumped out of bed, threw on his robe, and headed down to the kitchen to stop her before she set something on fire. What was she doing up at 1:00 a.m. anyway?

When he got to the kitchen, the flame under the kettle was off and Lexi was opening and closing cupboards. She was wearing that same long silk gown she'd worn in Greece, and all he could think about was getting her out of it.

"Looking for something?" he asked.

She spun around, startled. "What are you doing here?"

Her breasts swelled enticingly against the sheer fabric and he could see the rosy outline of her nipples. Maybe it was his imagination, but her chest looked fuller than it had just a week ago.

"Last I checked, I live here," he said. "What are *you* doing?"

"I couldn't sleep, so I came down to get something to drink."

"Were you looking for something?" he asked.

"Herbal tea," she said. "Sometimes it helps me sleep. I thought I might make a cup. Do you have any?"

"In the narrow cupboard above the coffeemaker." He watched, mesmerized once again by the sway of her hips under that silk as she crossed the kitchen and opened the cupboard. "Top shelf in the back."

She stretched for it, but even on her tiptoes she wasn't tall enough. She turned back to him and said, "I can't reach it."

He knew even before he took a step that he was going to regret this, but he couldn't stop himself. He crossed the kitchen, caging her into a corner, and to his surprise, she didn't object or try to move to one side. She smelled fantastic and she was giving off enough pheromones to bring a football team to its knees.

Resting one hand on the counter beside her, he reached up with the other to grab the box of tea bags. He told himself that getting this close to her without an audience was a bad idea, but the message was getting scrambled in his hormone-drenched brain. Instead of backing off, like he should have, his body was telling him to move closer.

Lexi's breathing sounded labored and he could feel her trembling. He wasn't sure if she was scared or excited, or a little bit of both.

"We shouldn't be doing this," she said, but she didn't try to stop him, didn't push him away.

"I know. But I get the feeling we're going to, anyway." He didn't just get the feeling, he knew for a fact.

She opened her mouth to speak, probably to tell him to back off, but since that was the last thing he wanted to hear, he lowered his head and kissed her instead. With his tongue in her mouth she wasn't able to do much but moan. Which was exactly what she did. Her arms went around his neck and she tunneled her fingers through his hair. If she'd been planning to stop him, she had obviously changed her mind. At this point, they were both too far gone to turn back, and he only felt slightly guilty for using her this way.

Wasn't it Lexi who had said that they both had needs, and suggested that since they were stuck with each other, why not have a little fun?

At that moment, he couldn't think of a single reason he shouldn't take her advice.

"Tell me you're not wearing panties under this," he said, gripping the silk in his hands.

She gave him a fiery smile. "Why don't you look and see?"

He pulled it up over her head. Nope, no panties. And damn did she look good naked.

"How about you?" she said, eyeing his robe. "Are you wearing anything under there?"

He grinned. "Why don't you look and find out?"

She undid the belt and shoved the robe off his shoulders, smiling when she realized he wasn't. For an instant, he considered carrying her up to his bedroom, but honestly, he didn't think he could wait that long. He wanted—needed—to be inside her. It hadn't even been a week since they'd last made love, but it felt like years.

Not love, he reminded himself. This was sex.

He lifted her up and set her on the counter. Without hesitation she hooked those long, shapely, perfect legs around his waist. He was inside her, buried just as far as he could go, before he even thought about using a condom.

But why bother? It wasn't as though he could get her more pregnant than she already was, right?

He wanted it to last, but she was so hot and wet and tight. The sensation of skin against skin had him hovering on the edge of a precipice, struggling to keep his balance, but Lexi was moaning and writhing and sinking her nails into his back. Then she gazed up at him with a look that was caught somewhere between shock and ecstasy, and her entire body started to tremble. Her muscles contracted around him and he couldn't have held back then if his life depended on it. He came so hard his knees nearly gave out and he had to grab the edge of the counter to hold himself up.

Lexi clung to him, her forehead resting on his chest, breathing hard. "We really shouldn't have done that."

"No," he said, his own breath coming in short rasps. "We probably shouldn't have."

He could always say the alcohol had impaired his judgment. What was her excuse?

She lifted her head and gazed up at him. "Now that we have that settled, you want to do it again?"

Eleven

Lexi woke the next morning at six-thirty and immediately felt that something was different. Something other than the fact that she was in Mitch's bed and she was curled up against his side while he slept soundly.

She lay there for several minutes, trying to put her finger on the change, then realized she didn't feel sick. She should be bolting to the bathroom by now, losing last night's dinner.

She lay there for another minute or two, sure that any second it would hit her, and still nothing.

Maybe she had to move a little, jostle her stomach, to get the ball rolling. She untangled herself from Mitch's arms and slowly pulled herself into a sitting position, waiting for that overwhelming wave of nausea, for the cold sweats and the abrupt rush of bile to her throat. Instead she felt something else in the pit of her stomach. She felt...*hungry*.

She usually couldn't choke anything down until closer to lunchtime, yet here it was not even seven and she was famished.

The doctor had told her chances were good the morning sickness would ease up, but she'd had no idea it would end so abruptly.

Mitch touched her back and in a groggy voice, asked, "Are you okay?"

"I think so." She had warned him last night, when he refused to let her get up and sleep in her own room, to expect her abrupt departure from bed.

He peered up at her through sleepy eyes, his hair adorably mussed. "Should I get you a bucket?"

She gave him a playful shove, even though she liked that he was worried about her. "I don't think that will be necessary. I actually feel pretty good. Like I could eat breakfast." Which meant he would have to make it since he'd asked that—until she started those lessons—she please not cook anything. Although she had managed to boil water last night without incident.

He looked over at the clock and groaned. "It's too early to eat."

"Don't you have to get up and get ready for work, anyway?"

"Since someone kept me up half the night, I was planning on sleeping in and going in late."

"*I* kept *you* up?"

"You were insatiable. I feel so…used."

She wasn't the one who kept dragging him back under the covers every time she tried to go back to her own room, or kiss her awake when she would start to doze off from sheer exhaustion. "You just keep telling yourself that," she said. "But we both know what really happened."

He grinned up at her. "Since you're not sick, how would you feel about it happening again, right now?"

She huffed impatiently, and said in her best exasperated voice, "I suppose breakfast can wait."

When he finally let her out of bed it was closer to lunchtime. She showered and dressed, and when she went downstairs to the kitchen to find him, he was fixing them something to eat. She had expected him to be in a suit, ready to go to the office, but he was dressed in casual slacks and a polo shirt.

"Don't you have to go to work?" she asked.

He shrugged and said, "They'll manage without me one more day. Besides, I promised you a driving lesson."

She had just figured, since he'd been intoxicated at the time, that he would have forgotten about the driving lessons. The thought of actually getting behind the wheel of a car, especially with Mitch watching, had her heart skipping a beat. "Maybe we shouldn't."

"How else will you learn?"

"What if I do it wrong?"

"You probably will at first, but that's all a part of the learning process."

"What if I do something terrible, like run us off an overpass or something?"

"I promise I'll keep you on solid ground until you get the hang of it."

She chewed her lip, wondering what she could say to talk him out of it without sounding like a total chicken.

Mitch reached over and took her hand. "Have a little faith in yourself, Lexi, and you'll do just fine."

That was the problem. She had been taught to believe that she couldn't do things on her own, but he was right. She had to stop being so afraid of everything, so willing to depend on other people. It was time she started living her life, and not just sitting back and watching the world pass by around her.

She took a deep breath and blew it out. "Okay. Let's do it."

"After we eat, we'll take you out for your first lesson."

At least this way she didn't have to ask Tara to do it.

Mitch's cell phone rang and he unclipped it from his belt to answer it. "Hey, Mark, what's up? Did they accept our offer?"

Lexi's heart jumped when she heard the real estate

agent's name. She held her breath while Mitch listened quietly, his expression hovering somewhere between curiosity and concern. He'd all but said he would do anything to get the house, but what if the owners changed their minds and refused to sell it?

"I understand," he said. "I'll talk to you later." He hung up and clipped the phone back on his belt. "That was Mark."

As if she hadn't already figured that out. "What did he say?"

"He heard from the seller."

"And?"

A slow smile spread across his face. "They accepted the offer. The house is ours."

Lexi screamed and threw herself into his arms. She had been so afraid that something would go wrong, she hadn't let herself hope it would really happen. Now she was so excited she could barely contain herself.

Mitch laughed and hugged her back. "I guess I don't have to ask if you're happy."

"I am," she said, resting her head against his chest, squeezing him tight. For the first time in a long time she was really, really happy.

Something had happened last night. When he took her hand and they walked into that party, something in their relationship had changed. She was sure of it. They could say that this marriage was nothing more than a business deal, but she knew it wasn't true. He was the man she'd spent that amazing week with in D.C., the one she had fallen in love with. And despite a few rocky patches, she knew that deep down she had never really stopped loving him. And he loved her, too, even if he hadn't said so.

"We close in a week," he said.

"We?" she asked, looking up at him.

"It's your house, too."

Her house. The idea made her almost giddy with excitement.

Everything was perfect. Even better than perfect.

Except for one thing. She still hadn't told Mitch the truth.

Lexi had assumed her lunch at the Cattleman's Club café would be just her and Kate, but when Tara dropped her off at the club and the hostess led her to the table, she saw that they were being joined by Summer Martindale, Cara Pettigrew-Novak, Alicia Montoya, and Rebecca Huntington.

Lexi wondered if she was walking straight into the lion's den. Kate had been incredibly sweet the other night at the party, but what if that had been an act? What if she resented the fact that Lexi had been engaged to her husband and she'd lured her here to humiliate her?

Kate saw Lexi approaching and rose from her chair, a huge smile on her face, and said, "Hey, sister-in-law!" Then she proceeded to wrap Lexi up in one of those warm and affectionate hugs.

Well, that was unexpected.

"Sit down," Kate said, gesturing to the empty seat beside hers. "I think you know everyone here."

As she sat, the women smiled and greeted her warmly, and Lexi began to think that maybe this would just be a friendly lunch with the girls after all. Which for her would be a totally new experience. She hadn't been allowed to have many friends or associate with people who weren't the top shelf of society—she couldn't have contact with anyone who could be a potential danger to her father's political aspirations. He never would have approved of a friendship with someone like Kate, a lowly assistant, or a dancer like Cara. In fact, there wasn't a single person at the table, besides Rebecca Huntington maybe, whom he would deem acceptable. And for the first time in her life, she didn't care what he thought. Lately, the past couple of days especially, she'd been feeling rebellious and independent, and she *liked* it.

A waitress appeared at their table to take Lexi's drink order. Lexi saw that everyone else had an alcoholic beverage, and boy did she wish she could have one, too, but she ordered an iced tea instead. For a second, she worried someone might question her choice, but no one said a word.

"We try to meet at least once a month," Cara told her, "so we can discuss all of the latest gossip."

Lexi wondered if she had ever been the topic of conversation.

"Today we're also celebrating," Summer said, and all heads turned her way.

"What are we celebrating?" Alicia asked.

Summer held out her left hand, so everyone could see the enormous diamond ring and diamond-encrusted wedding band she was wearing. "Darius and I eloped!"

Excited squeals and congratulations followed.

"I'm so jealous!" Rebecca said. "It seems as though everyone is getting married but me."

"Marriage is hard work," Cara said, then added with a smile, "but well worth it when you finally get the gears running smoothly."

The waitress brought Lexi's tea and set a basket of fresh bread and rolls on the table. Lexi was absolutely famished—the last few days it seemed as though she was constantly eating—so she dove right in and grabbed a roll.

"What's the latest with the refinery fire?" Rebecca asked Summer, and Lexi couldn't help noticing that everyone glanced at Alicia. At first she wondered why, then remembered that it was Alicia's brother Alex who was being looked at for the arson.

"Is Darius any closer to finding out who did it?" Kate asked.

Summer shrugged apologetically. "He doesn't say too much about his work."

"I know what everyone thinks," Alicia said. "But Alex would never hurt a soul. He didn't set that fire."

"I believe you," Rebecca told her. "Alex is a good person." Lexi noticed that the woman looked at Rebecca with surprise. "Based on what I've heard, I mean," she added, blushing slightly.

"What about the rezoning in the Somerset district?" Kate asked. "I heard Alex was behind it."

"He is, because someone had to do something to pick up revenue. I know that no one wants to believe it, but the town is in trouble," said Alicia. "With Alex's help, I'm working on a project to create an 'Old Towne' tourist attraction downtown. It will bring jobs and add tourist revenue to the city, not to mention preserve history, which, as curator of the museum, is important to me."

"Sounds like your life lately has been all work and no play?" Cara asked with a strange smile on her face.

"Well, not *all* work," Alicia said cryptically.

"Did you meet someone?" Rebecca asked excitedly.

Alicia flashed them a smile. "Maybe."

"Girlfriend, are you holding out on us?" Summer asked.

"Let's just say I'm afraid I'm going to jinx it. But I will say that I have a date this Friday. He said he wants to take me somewhere special."

"You have to come to Sweet Nothings," Rebecca insisted. "A special date deserves sexy underwear."

Alicia laughed. "I could spend my entire salary in your store, Becca."

"You're one of those people who can eat anything and still stay pick thin, aren't you?" Cara said. Lexi was surprised to find that Cara was talking to her, and mortified when she realized why. While everyone had been chatting, Lexi had almost wiped out the bread basket by herself.

"Sorry," she said, setting down the roll she'd been devouring. She could feel her cheeks turning pink. "I skipped breakfast."

"I just have to look at food and my butt gets bigger," Rebecca said.

"I hate to think what I'd look like if I weren't dancing all the time," Cara said.

After that, Lexi was careful not to draw attention to herself. She ordered a salad with the dressing on the side, then only ate half, even though she was hungry enough to eat three times that much. Maybe the next time they met—if she was even invited next time—she would be able to tell them about the baby.

It was getting to the point where she *had* to tell Mitch the truth. She had almost said it the other day after they found the house, but she'd chickened out at the last minute. She knew, though, that it was time. She'd begun to believe that now he would be thrilled to learn that the baby was his. Because even though he hadn't said it out loud yet, Lexi was convinced that he loved her. He showed her every day in a hundred little ways. Most of them in the bedroom.

Though she knew better than to mistake sex for love, she was sure that this time it was different.

The alternative was no longer an option.

Twelve

Mitch found it ironic that when he had agreed to meet at Darius's office, he'd figured he would be thankful for the time away from his wife, when in reality, he would much rather be at home with her. For a self-proclaimed workaholic who loved his job above all else, he'd been taking a lot of time off since they got back from Greece.

At first he tried to convince himself that it was just the sex, and then he told himself that he felt guilty leaving her alone, or was worried that she might try to use the stove and burn his house down. But now, as he sat in the conference room of Darius's security firm with Darius, Lance, Kevin and Justin, he couldn't deny that he simply missed her company.

As hard as he tried to tell himself that she was a spoiled, heartless brat who cared about no one but herself, her actions said he was way off base. If what she'd told him about her father was true, and after seeing the senator in action he was pretty damned sure it was, it was a miracle that Lexi had any self-esteem at all. He now believed that she hadn't hopped from his bed to his brother's as some sort of vendetta, but because she was desperate to be accepted and loved. She *deserved* to be with someone who could love her. But Mitch didn't do love.

In a few weeks, he'd gone from thinking that he was somehow superior to her, a better human being, to thinking that he just didn't measure up. But he had to stick it out for the baby's sake, the niece or nephew growing in her who deserved to be raised by family, not some stranger.

"So, when is this meeting going to start?" Kevin asked Darius.

"As soon as the last person I invited gets here." No sooner had the words left his mouth than the conference-room door opened and Alex Montoya walked in.

In an instant, Lance was up and out of his chair. "What is he doing here?"

Alex shot Lance daggers with his eyes.

"I asked him to come," Darius said. "As a Cattleman Club member, this concerns him, too."

Mitch sat up in his chair, in case he needed to hold his brother back, but after a tense moment, Lance took his seat and Alex found a chair on the opposite side of the table. Mitch didn't like Alex, but he gave him credit for having the guts to show his face.

"I called you all here," Darius said, "because I have suspicions that someone may be cooking the club books."

"Are you suggesting that someone is embezzling from the club?" Justin asked.

"That's exactly what I think."

"What led you to think that?" Kevin asked.

"When I set up the new billing system for Helping Hands, something strange happened. The club cut us a check for expenses, but it was made out to Helping Hearts. I called the office and talked to Sebastian Huntington and asked him to fix the error. I just assumed he'd used the wrong name, but he said that he'd sent the wrong check by accident."

"I didn't know there was an organization named Helping Hearts," Mitch said, although admittedly, he didn't pay much attention to the club's finances.

"I didn't either," Darius said. "But I was curious so I did a bit of research, and after some digging, I found that Helping Hearts doesn't exist."

"As club members we have the right to examine the books," Alex said, looking as concerned as the rest of them.

"I suppose you think you should be the one to investigate," Lance snapped back. "How do we know you're not the one behind it?"

Alex glared at him. "First you call me an arsonist, now you accuse me of theft? Perhaps you would like to blame me for the stock market crash as well."

"I know," Darius interrupted, before fists started flying, "that it can't feasibly be someone in this room. Only a member higher up in the ranks could pull this off."

"Like who?" Kevin asked.

"I'm not ready to point any fingers yet. And Alex is right, we need someone to examine the books. I think that person should be Mitch."

Suddenly all eyes were on him. "Why me?"

"I can handle setting up a simple billing system," Darius told him, "but you're the financial whiz kid of the group. If anyone would be able to spot discrepancies, it's you."

"I agree," Justin said.

"I do, as well," Alex agreed, which earned him a sharp look from Lance.

Kevin added his vote. "Me, too."

"So it's unanimous," Lance said.

Mitch wasn't sure if he was comfortable with this, but it seemed he didn't have much choice. "And if I find something?"

"We'll demand an audit from an outside firm. According to the bylaws, the club has no choice but to comply."

"I'm still having a tough time believing someone would steal from the club," Kevin said.

"So was I," Darius assured him. "I never would have come forward with this if I wasn't sure. You'll keep us posted, Mitch?"

"Of course."

The meeting broke up after that, Alex wisely being the first one to leave. On his way out, Justin asked Mitch, "You want to head to the club for a drink? Watch some soccer?"

Normally, Mitch wouldn't have hesitated to spend a few hours with his best friend, but he didn't feel right leaving Lexi alone. Besides, he had promised they would talk about contractors and the renovations they wanted to make on the house. "I can't tonight," he told Justin.

"Have to get back to the old ball and chain?"

Mitch didn't justify that with a response, he just shot Justin a look.

Justin laughed and shook his head. "Damn. I never thought I'd see the day when Mitchell Brody settled down."

"You could be next," Mitch said, which only made Justin laugh harder.

"I wouldn't advise holding your breath. Now that you're tied down, that just means more available women for me."

Leave it to Justin to rationalize it out like that. Although it surprised Mitch to realize it, he didn't miss playing the field. Maybe later that would change and he would begin to feel restless. But for now he was quite content being a one-woman man.

When Lexi answered the knock at the front door, the last person she expected to see standing on the porch was her father. As far as she knew, he was supposed to be in D.C.

"Daddy, what are you doing here?"

"I need to speak with you," he said, entering without waiting for an invitation.

"Of course," she replied, stepping aside. Maybe he was here to apologize for the way he'd acted at the party.

He gazed around the foyer looking unimpressed. Probably not big or grand enough for him. "Is your husband here?"

"No, he had a meeting." She gestured toward the kitchen. "I was just making myself a cup of tea. Would you like one?"

"You're making it? Does your husband not even have the decency to hire a housekeeper?"

She shrugged. "It's not a big deal. In fact, I sort of like doing things myself for a change."

He shook his head. "It's even worse than I thought."

Clearly that apology wasn't going to happen. "What's worse than you thought?"

"Your life. What Mitch has reduced you to."

Reduced her to? On the contrary, it felt as though

she had been introduced to a world she never knew existed, with opportunities and possibilities she had never dreamed of. "I'm fine, Daddy. Really."

"Nothing about this is 'fine.' After the degrading display the other night at the party, I've decided not to give the Brody brothers my support."

Her heart sank. "You can't do that."

"I can and I will. I still can't believe the way he was groping you. Do you have any idea how it looked to everyone else in the room?"

"Probably like we were a newlywed couple so madly in love we couldn't stand being apart."

"Well, the charade is over, so there's no need for you to stay here any longer. Pack your things and I'll take you home."

She didn't want to leave. "You promised them your support."

"I also told him that if he hurt you, I would crush him."

She began feeling a little frantic. Her father was being completely unreasonable. "But he *didn't* hurt me."

"He sullied your reputation, which is even worse, as far as I'm concerned."

"Reputation is more important than my happiness? I love Mitch."

He spit out a rueful laugh, and regarded her as though she were the village idiot. "You can't possibly be that naive. He only married you for my support."

The lengths he would go to, the things he would say to make her feel bad about herself, knew no bounds. But she knew exactly what this was about, even if he wouldn't admit it. It had nothing to do with reputation or Mitch's behavior at the party. He only wanted her to leave Mitch because she wanted to stay. He wanted control of her life back. Married to Mitch, he could no longer manipulate her. But this time she didn't have to listen to him. "You really can't stand it, can you?"

"Stand what?"

"To see me happy."

He scoffed. "That's ridiculous."

"Then why would you say something like that to me? I say I love Mitch and you accuse him of using me?"

"I said it because it's true. You know that I've never believed in coddling you."

"How do you know Mitch hasn't fallen in love with me?"

He shook his head sadly, as though she were even more pathetic than he realized.

"Do you believe I'm that horrible?" she asked. "That unlovable?"

"I didn't say that. But he isn't right for you."

"A month ago you seemed to think he was."

"Well, I was wrong."

If he couldn't accept that Mitch loved her, that was his problem, not hers. Mitch was going to be furious when he found out that her father had reneged on their deal, but she was pretty confident that he wouldn't hold it against her.

"Charade or not, I can't end the marriage."

"Why not?"

She shouldn't say it, but as soon as she told Mitch the truth everyone would know anyway. "I'm pregnant."

"Pregnant?" The anger disappeared and to her surprise, a look of wonder overwhelmed his face. "I'm going to be a grandfather?"

She had expected him to be furious. But it made sense that he would approve now that he was getting something he wanted out of the deal. And he had always wanted a grandson.

She smiled and nodded.

"That's...incredible."

"We had even discussed naming him after you," she said, even though they had done no such thing. They didn't have a clue what the baby's gender would be, much less what they planned to name it.

But he seemed to buy it because he beamed with pride. "I suppose a divorce *is* out of the question now, but we can figure out a way to make it work."

She smiled, thinking it was time to go for the throat. "You can start by giving Mitch and Lance all the senatorial support they need."

His smile faded. "I can't do that."

"You will if you want to see your grandchild."

He was so stunned that for a moment, he didn't seem to know what to say. It was the first time she had ever seen him rendered speechless and she enjoyed every second of it. When he found his voice, he asked, his tone soaked in disbelief, "You would use your own child against me?"

She sighed. "If I have to. Of course, I have plenty of other things I could hold against you."

"What things?"

"Things that could make your life very difficult when you're trying to get reelected."

The color leached from his face. "Did you just threaten to blackmail me?"

She sure as hell did. For the first time in her life she stood up to him and it felt wonderful. She flashed him a "Bless your Heart" smile. "Daddy, blackmail sounds so…uncivilized. Up on Capitol Hill I believe they call it extortion."

"I can't believe you would do this to me."

She shrugged. "I guess you could say that I learned from the master."

She waited for the anger, for him to explode, but to her surprise, it didn't happen. He just stood there, perplexed, as though he simply could not grasp what had just happened. That his compliant little girl had finally grown a will of her own. God knows it was about damned time. Then the front door opened and Mitch walked through, the vestiges of a cool early-autumn breeze following him inside.

"I thought that was your car outside," he said to her father as he walked right past him without shaking his hand or anything, pulling Lexi into his arms and kissing her. "Sorry it took so long, sweetheart."

Long? He'd barely been gone an hour. She had assumed "meeting" meant maybe twenty minutes of business followed by a few hours of drinking and bullshitting with the guys. Sort of like her lunch with Kate, but with more profanity and testosterone.

"Daddy stopped in to say hello," she told him. "Wasn't that nice?"

He obviously knew something was up, and he played along, saying in a Southern drawl that she had never heard him use before, "Why, yes it was. Can I get you a drink, Senator?"

"Unfortunately, he was just leaving," Lexi said. "But thanks for stopping by, Daddy."

Looking shell-shocked and confused, her father mumbled goodbye and let himself out of the house. As soon as he was gone, Mitch turned to her and, the drawl gone, asked, "What the hell just happened?"

Thirteen

Mitch lay in bed several hours later, Lexi against his side, her body warm and soft. He couldn't stop smiling. "I wish I could have seen the look on his face when you threatened him. That must have been priceless."

"I keep waiting to feel guilty. I never dreamed of saying something like that to him. Instead, I feel…liberated."

"I don't mean for this to sound condescending, but I'm proud of you," he said, and he could feel her smile.

"I'm proud of me, too. And I don't think you ever have to worry about losing his support. It's a real possibility that he won't ever speak to me again, though."

"How do you feel about that?"

"Not as bad as I expected. In a way, I kind of feel relieved. I don't need him anymore." She was quiet for a moment, then said, "Mitch, there's something I need to tell you. Two things, actually."

He rolled on his side to look at her. "What?"

"First, I lied to you. I said something really awful that wasn't true."

He frowned. "What?"

"It was the morning after we slept together in D.C. I thought…" She paused and bit her lip.

"You thought what?"

She took a deep breath. "I was so naive. I woke up, and I thought that you were going to beg me to marry you instead of Lance. I thought you…loved me. And you have no idea how long I'd waited for someone to feel that way about me. But the first thing you said that morning was that sleeping together had been a mistake. I was crushed. I lashed out and said the most awful thing I could think of."

"That you used me?"

She nodded.

In an odd way he was relieved, and at the same time it disturbed him. Not because she lied—he understood why she'd done it, and couldn't really blame her—but because she had just cemented the fact that he had totally misjudged her.

"I know we had barely spent a week together, but I loved you, Mitch. And I think…I think I still do."

He knew what she wanted, what she desperately

needed, but as much as he wanted her to be happy, he couldn't bring himself to lie to her. "I care for you, Lexi. I really do. I just can't…"

She rolled onto her back, but not before he saw her face fall, her happiness crumble. "I understand."

"It's not you. It's me."

She shrugged. "You don't have to explain."

He waited for her to get angry, or to cry. To do something. But she just lay there quietly and he felt like the world's biggest heel. She deserved better than this. Better than him. She should be with someone who loved her. Who was capable of love.

"What else?" he asked.

"What do you mean?"

"You said there were two things you had to tell me."

"Oh," she said softly, turning away from him to lie on her side, pulling the covers up over her shoulder. "It wasn't important."

He considered pushing the issue, but figured maybe he was best off not knowing. He lay awake for what felt like hours, marinating in his own guilt and self-loathing.

When he woke in the morning and reached for Lexi, she wasn't there. He got out of bed and pulled on his robe. He figured Lexi was downstairs in the kitchen making tea, but he found her in her bedroom, packing. She was leaving him.

He was more disappointed than surprised. "Going somewhere?" he asked.

She turned to him, looking tired and sad. "Good morning."

He doubted that. "You don't have to do this."

"Yes, I do."

He had half a mind to beg her to stay, to swear that things would change, but that would just be cruel and selfish. The best thing he could do for Lexi was let her go.

"Are you going back to your father?"

"God, no. I would never give him the satisfaction."

"Good. He doesn't deserve you. And don't worry about money. I'll see that you and the baby are set for life."

"I appreciate that, but I can't spend the rest of my life with other people always taking care of me. I need to do this on my own."

"Where will you go?"

"Tara said I can stay with her until I'm on my feet."

He was tempted to insist that she stay with him, at least until the baby was born. By then, the house would be ready and she could stay there. But if she needed to prove something to herself, he wasn't going to stop her. Maybe she would realize how hard it was to be on her own, and come back to him.

But Lexi was tough, and he had the feeling she would be just fine. He would miss her, and always care about her, but the truth was she deserved a better man than Mitch Brody, and he hoped someday she would find him.

* * *

Lexi had never been so humiliated in her life.

Her father had been right all along. Mitch didn't love her. He "cared" for her, which she was pretty sure translated into caring about her father's senatorial support. Just as her father had warned her.

She could be a bitch about it and see that her father did everything in his power to crush them, but she just wasn't the vindictive type. After all, it wasn't Mitch's fault that Lexi had fallen in love with him. She had done that herself, creating her own fantasy world. Mitch had told her time and time again that their marriage was just business, but she hadn't listened.

"You have to tell him the truth," Tara said, handing her a steaming cup of tea. She took a seat in the armchair across from the couch where Lexi sat. "It's his baby. He deserves to be a part of its life."

"I will tell him. Eventually."

"When? After the kid is out of college?"

"After I get back on my feet, when I don't need his help." Which might be a while considering she had no job skills, no driver's license and all she'd had the will to do the past four days was sit curled up on the couch in Tara's condo, feeling sorry for herself.

The prospect of supporting herself and the baby was beyond overwhelming, but she was determined to figure out a way.

"He's going to have to pay child support," Tara said.

She knew that was inevitable. He would insist, because that's the kind of man he was. But she wasn't ready to accept his help. Not yet. Although at this point, there was no way he would be anything but furious with her when he found out the baby was his, and he would be completely justified. She should have told him the truth that day he assumed the baby was Lance's, whether he believed her or not. At least then she could say that she'd been honest. But she had procrastinated and put it off and painted herself into a tiny little corner that she had no hope of getting out of unscathed.

When all was said and done, everything was her fault. She had made this mess, done this to herself, and she was the only one who could fix it.

But right now, she just wasn't ready.

Mitch sat in his office, staring out the window, finding it impossible to concentrate on his work. Since Lexi had left him, he hadn't been able to think straight. Hell, he'd barely been able to function. He just couldn't stop thinking about her, *missing* her. He'd stripped his bed and pillows, even sprayed air freshener, but he could still smell her, still feel her presence in the room. He couldn't drive his car without picturing her behind the wheel, so adorably nervous, but determined to learn. He couldn't walk into the kitchen without remembering the night they had made love there.

He had lost all interest in buying the house. Part

of what had drawn him to it was her excitement, the thought of them being a family. Now there didn't seem much point in leaving his townhouse, even though he was miserable whenever he was there.

She had been indelibly ingrained in every part of his life, and he couldn't help wondering if this feeling he was having, the crushing ache, the longing he felt every time he thought of her—which was pretty much all the time—meant he loved her.

"Why don't you just call her?"

Mitch turned to find Lance standing in the doorway, arms folded across his chest. He sighed and asked, "Is it that obvious?"

Lance grinned. "You look just like I felt when Kate left me. And trust me when I say, if she loves you, she'll forgive whatever you did."

Lance was a good brother. He had always been there to protect Mitch, had always taken care of him and supported him no matter what. He owed him the truth. He'd already waited too long. "Come in, and close the door."

Lance did as he asked. "What's going on?"

"Lexi is pregnant," he said.

Lance laughed. "Already? You two sure didn't waste any time."

"It's not what you think. The baby…it's not mine."

He frowned. "What do you mean, it's not yours?"

"She's more than three months."

"Three months? That would mean she got

pregnant…" He trailed off, so Mitch finished the sentence for him.

"Right around the time you two were engaged."

He shook his head in disbelief. "Son of a bitch. All that time I felt so guilty for going behind her back with Kate, and she was cheating on *me?*"

His brother could not be that dense. "She wasn't cheating on you, you idiot. The baby is yours."

Instead of looking shocked or humbled, or even angry, Lance laughed and said, "No, it isn't."

He must have been in some serious denial. "Yes, Lance. It is. She told me herself."

"Then she was lying."

"How can you know that for sure?"

"Easy. Because I never slept with her."

"What?"

"I only kissed her once and believe me when I say that it wasn't all that red hot for either of us."

"Then why, on my honeymoon, did you tell me that if I slept with her it wouldn't be a disappointment?"

He shrugged. "A guess. It wasn't, was it?"

"Of course not, but…" This didn't make any sense. "Why would she tell me it was you if…?" Realization hit him with a force that knocked the breath from his lungs. "Oh, shit."

He must have gone white as death, because Lance asked, "Jesus, Mitch, what's wrong?"

How could he have been so stupid? "I'm an ass, that's what's wrong."

"I'm sorry, but you've completely lost me."

Despite what he'd believed at first, he knew without a doubt that Lexi hadn't been capable of hopping from Mitch's bed to Lance's. And that could only mean one thing.

"It's mine," he said, and at his brother's confused look added, "The baby. Lexi is having *my* baby."

"Then why did she tell you it was mine?"

"She didn't. When she told me she was pregnant, I just assumed it was yours."

Lance looked more confused than ever. "I thought you said she was three months. How could it be yours?"

Mitch dropped his head in his hands. He had no choice but to tell Lance the truth. He looked up at his big brother. His protector. "There's something I have to tell you. Something I should have told you months ago."

"What?" Lance asked.

"Remember that week I spent with Lexi on your behalf?"

Lance nodded. "Of course."

"That last night, before you proposed, we… I slept with her." Mitch waited for the impending explosion.

"I'm not an idiot," Lance said calmly. "I saw the way you two acted after the D.C. trip. I kind of figured something happened."

Mitch couldn't believe that Lance knew, or at least suspected, this entire time. "You're not mad?"

"It wasn't a real engagement."

"But you're my brother. You were going to marry her."

"But I didn't. If it would make you feel better, I could punch you again. Although it looks like you're doing a pretty fair job of beating yourself up."

"I deserve worse, believe me."

"Let me get this straight. She told you she was pregnant, and you just automatically assumed it was mine?"

He nodded.

"So, what you were saying to her was that you believed she slept with you, then turned around and hopped in the sack with your brother?"

Mitch pinched the bridge of his nose. "Yeah, pretty much." Lexi must have been furious. Not to mention humiliated.

"Why didn't she just tell you the truth?"

"She probably thought I wouldn't believe her."

"Would you have believed her?"

"Probably not."

"I hate to say this, Mitch, but you are an ass."

He wanted to be furious with Lexi for not telling him the truth, for lying by omission, but the only person he could muster any anger for was himself. All of this, this entire jumbled-up mess, was his fault. Yes, Lexi had lied about using him, but he had spent a week wining and dining her, and yes, seducing her, only to turn around and say it was a mistake. Could he really blame her for being hurt and lashing out? If he had known her better then, he would have realized she wasn't capable of what she'd claimed. She would never use anyone.

Ironically, if he had been honest with his brother from the start, he would have learned the truth and they could have avoided this entire mess.

"What I still don't get is how she got pregnant," Mitch said.

His brother smirked. "You don't really need me to explain that to you, do you, Mitch?"

Mitch sighed. "I know how, I'm just not sure when it could have happened. We were careful."

Lance shrugged. "Birth control has been known to fail."

"I think… I think I love her."

"You think?"

No. He knew he loved her. It was the only explanation for how miserable he was without her. He rose from his chair. "I have to go see her."

"It's about time."

Mitch grabbed his jacket and headed for the door. Then he remembered there was a slight hitch to his plan. He had no idea where she was.

Lance must have read his mind because he said, "She's staying at her assistant's condo." Mitch looked confused. "Wives are an excellent source of information."

Hopefully, Mitch would be finding that out for himself. He was going to ask Lexi to marry him, and this time they were going to do it right.

Fourteen

The doorbell rang, and since Lexi was home alone and not expecting anyone, she peered out the front window to see who was standing on the porch. Her breath caught and her heart started to hammer a million miles an hour when she saw that it was Mitch.

What could he possibly want?

He must have come right from work because he was wearing a suit. He glanced her way and though she dropped the curtain, she wasn't fast enough. He saw her.

Damn it!

He knocked on the door and called, "Come on, Lexi, I need to talk to you."

She was going to shout back that everything they needed to say had been said, but it was a lie. Instead, she unlocked the door and pulled it open. "What?"

"I finally figured it out."

"Figured what out?" she asked, stepping aside so he could come in.

"When it happened."

She shut the door and turned to him. "When what happened?"

"When you got pregnant."

His words nearly stopped her heart. She hoped he didn't mean what she thought he meant. "W-when?"

"The third time, in the middle of the night. For a few minutes we didn't use a condom. Am I right?"

Stunned, she asked, "How did you…?"

"I figured it was time to tell my brother the truth. Imagine his surprise when he found out that he was having a child with a woman he never slept with."

She chewed her lip. "I never actually said—"

"That you slept with him. I know."

"I was going to tell you—"

"But you didn't trust me," he finished for her. "I get it. I was an ass."

Huh? What was he saying? "You're not angry?" Lexi asked.

"How can I be angry at you when this entire mess is my fault?"

What? This was her fault. "This whole thing started because I lied and said I used you."

"Lexi, this whole thing started because *I* told *you* we made a mistake, because I didn't want to admit that I was falling in love with you."

He *loved* her?

No, of course he didn't. She knew exactly what this was. Now that he knew about the baby, he wanted them to be together. Or maybe he was worried that he and Lance would lose the senator's support. Either way, it was obvious he would say anything to get his way, even if that meant lying about loving her.

"Aren't you going to say anything?" he asked.

"Like what?"

"Hell, I don't know, maybe something like, you love me, too?"

"I won't stay with you just for the baby's sake."

"I don't recall asking you to. This is entirely selfish. I want you to stay with me for my sake. Because I love you."

"If you're worried about losing my father's support, I'll see to it that you don't."

"This has nothing to do with that. As far as I'm concerned, he can take his support and shove it where the sun don't shine."

"I don't believe you. It's the only reason you married me."

"Maybe it was," he admitted. "But it's not why I want to marry you now."

"We're already married."

"I know, but I was thinking that it would be nice if we had a big wedding, did it right."

"No. What would be nice is a neat and tidy divorce."

He folded his arms across his chest. "You still honestly think I'm doing this for your father's support?"

"Among other things."

"You don't believe I love you?"

She shook her head.

"Okay," he said. "I guess I'm just going to have to prove it to you."

Good luck with that.

He pulled out his cell phone, dialed a number and put it on speaker.

"Who are you calling?" she asked. If she wouldn't believe him, did he think she would believe someone else?

"Senator Cavanaugh's office," she heard her father's secretary say.

"It's Mitch Brody, could I speak with the senator? It's urgent."

"One moment, Mr. Brody." She put him on hold.

"What are you doing?" she asked.

"They say actions speak louder than words."

Oh, no. He wouldn't.

Her father came on the line, his tone exasperated. "What do you want, Brody?"

"Hello, Senator, I just wanted to tell you to take you support and sh—"

"Mitch!" she screeched. She snatched the phone away from him and snapped it shut. "Are you crazy?"

"No. I love you."

His phone immediately began to ring, but Lexi ignored it. "Why would you do that?"

"How many times are you going to make me say it? It isn't about the baby, and it's not about the senator. You could be carrying the postman's baby and I would still love you. And my business, my life, means nothing if you aren't in it."

Would he say all that if he didn't really mean it? If he didn't love her?

"You love *me?*" she asked.

"Yes, *you.* You know, we really have to work on this self-esteem issue you have."

She bit her lip and nodded, afraid that if she said anything, she would burst into tears. Mitch must have realized, because he pulled her into his arms and held her. She could hardly believe it was real— that after everything they had been through, this was actually going to work out.

"You know, you could say it, too," he said.

She smiled up at him. "I love you, Mitch. I've known since that week in D.C. that I wanted to spend the rest of my life with you."

He gazed at her, his eyes so full of love and affection she had to swallow back a sob. He caressed her cheek and said, "I can hardly wait for us to be a family."

Tears slipped from the corners of her eyes and he brushed them away with his thoughts.

"Those better be happy tears," he said.

She grinned up at him. "Absolutely."

He grinned and kissed the tip of her nose. "We had kind of a bumpy start, I guess."

"A little," she said, but she knew that from now, it would only get better.

* * * * *

Don't miss the next book in our
Texas Cattleman's Club series,
THE MAVERICK'S VIRGIN MISTRESS,
available next month
from Silhouette Desire.

*Celebrate 60 years of pure reading
pleasure with Harlequin®!*

To commemorate the event, Silhouette Special
Edition invites you to Ashley O'Ballivan's bed-
and-breakfast in the small town of Stone
Creek. The beautiful innkeeper will have her
hands full caring for her old flame Jack
McCall. He's on the run and recovering from
a mysterious illness, but that won't stop him
from trying to win Ashley back.

*Enjoy an exclusive glimpse of Linda Lael Miller's
AT HOME IN STONE CREEK
Available in November 2009
from Silhouette Special Edition®.*

The helicopter swung abruptly sideways in a dizzying arch, setting Jack McCall's fever-ravaged brain spinning.

His friend's voice sounded tinny, coming through the earphones. "You belong in a hospital," he said. "Not some backwater bed-and-breakfast."

All Jack really knew about the virus raging through his system was that it wasn't contagious, and there was no known treatment for it besides a lot of rest and quiet. "I don't like hospitals," he responded, hoping he sounded like his normal self. "They're full of sick people."

Vince Griffin chuckled but it was a dry sound, rough at the edges. "What's in Stone Creek,

Arizona?" he asked. "Besides a whole lot of nothin'?"

Ashley O'Ballivan was in Stone Creek, and she was a whole lot of somethin', but Jack had neither the strength nor the inclination to explain. After the way he'd ducked out six months before, he didn't expect a welcome, knew he didn't deserve one. But Ashley, being Ashley, would take him in whatever her misgivings.

He had to get to Ashley; he'd be all right.

He closed his eyes, letting the fever swallow him.

There was no telling how much time had passed when he became aware of the chopper blades slowing overhead. Dimly, he saw the private ambulance waiting on the airfield outside of Stone Creek; it seemed that twilight had descended.

Jack sighed with relief. His clothes felt clammy against his flesh. His teeth began to chatter as two figures unloaded a gurney from the back of the ambulance and waited for the blades to stop.

"Great," Vince remarked, unsnapping his seat belt. "Those two look like volunteers, not real EMTs."

The chopper bounced sickeningly on its runners, and Vince, with a shake of his head, pushed open his door and jumped to the ground, head down.

Jack waited, wondering if he'd be able to stand on his own. After fumbling unsuccessfully with the buckle on his seat belt, he decided not.

When it was safe the EMTs approached, following Vince, who opened Jack's door.

His old friend Tanner Quinn stepped around Vince, his grin not quite reaching his eyes.

"You look like hell warmed over," he told Jack cheerfully.

"Since when are you an EMT?" Jack retorted.

Tanner reached in, wedged a shoulder under Jack's right arm and hauled him out of the chopper. His knees immediately buckled, and Vince stepped up, supporting him on the other side.

"In a place like Stone Creek," Tanner replied, "everybody helps out."

They reached the wheeled gurney, and Jack found himself on his back.

Tanner and the second man strapped him down, a process that brought back a few bad memories.

"Is there even a hospital in this place?" Vince asked irritably from somewhere in the night.

"There's a pretty good clinic over in Indian Rock," Tanner answered easily, "and it isn't far to Flagstaff." He paused to help his buddy hoist Jack and the gurney into the back of the ambulance. "You're in good hands, Jack. My wife is the best veterinarian in the state."

Jack laughed raggedly at that.

Vince muttered a curse.

Tanner climbed into the back beside him, perched on some kind of fold-down seat. The other man shut the doors.

"You in any pain?" Tanner said as his partner climbed into the driver's seat and started the engine.

"No." Jack looked up at his oldest and closest friend and wished he'd listened to Vince. Ever since he'd come down with the virus—a week after snatching a five-year-old girl back from her non-custodial parent, a small-time Colombian drug dealer—he hadn't been able to think about anyone or anything but Ashley. When he *could* think, anyway.

Now, in one of the first clearheaded moments he'd experienced since checking himself out of Bethesda the day before, he realized he might be making a major mistake. Not by facing Ashley—he owed her that much and a lot more. No, he could be putting her in danger, putting Tanner and his daughter and his pregnant wife in danger, too.

"I shouldn't have come here," he said, keeping his voice low.

Tanner shook his head, his jaw clamped down hard as though he was irritated by Jack's statement.

"This is where you belong," Tanner insisted. "If you'd had sense enough to know that six months ago, old buddy, when you bailed on Ashley without so much as a fare-thee-well, you wouldn't be in this mess."

Ashley. The name had run through his mind a million times in those six months, but hearing somebody say it out loud was like having a fist close around his insides and squeeze hard.

Jack couldn't speak.

Tanner didn't press for further conversation.

The ambulance bumped over country roads, finally hitting smooth blacktop.

"Here we are," Tanner said. "Ashley's place."

* * * * *

Will Jack be able to patch things up with Ashley, or will his past put the woman he loves in harm's way?

Find out in
AT HOME IN STONE CREEK
by Linda Lael Miller.
Available November 2009
from Silhouette Special Edition®.

**This November,
Silhouette Special Edition®
brings you**

NEW YORK TIMES
BESTSELLING AUTHOR

LINDA LAEL MILLER

At Home in
Stone Creek

*Available in November
wherever books are sold.*